Maddy went into
down on the pa
desire to make th
back upstairs to
head.

Shakily, she dialed Mickey's number.

She breathed a sigh of relief when Mickey answered. "Hi, Mickey. It's Maddy. You called me?"

That was dumb, she scolded herself. Surely he must remember that he called her. But Mickey didn't seem to notice anything amiss. "Yeah. I'm having trouble with that math assignment, and I know it's your best subject."

Maddy was pleased that Mickey had remembered. "Do you want me to try to explain it to you?" she asked.

"Yeah, that would be great."

They both got out their math books and Maddy tried to talk Mickey through the problems. Tentatively, she asked if he wanted to come over. "Maybe it would be easier if I could actually show you how to do the equations."

There were a few seconds of silence, and Maddy thought she had blown it. Then Mickey said, "What time's good for you?"

Any time, Maddy thought dreamily.

BY ILENE COOPER

Books about <u>The Holiday Five</u>:

Trick or Trouble?

The Worst Noel

The <u>Hollywood Wars</u> series:

My Co-Star, My Enemy

Lights, Camera, Attitude

Seeing Red

Trouble in Paradise

THE HOLIDAY FIVE

Stupid Cupid

BY ILENE COOPER

PUFFIN BOOKS

PUFFIN BOOKS
Published by the Penguin Group
Penguin Books USA Inc., 375 Hudson Street, New York, New York 10014, U.S.A.
Penguin Books Ltd, 27 Wrights Lane, London W8 5TZ, England
Penguin Books Australia Ltd, Ringwood, Victoria, Australia
Penguin Books Canada Ltd, 10 Alcorn Avenue, Toronto, Ontario, Canada M4V 3B2
Penguin Books (N.Z.) Ltd, 182-190 Wairau Road, Auckland 10, New Zealand

Penguin Books Ltd, Registered Offices: Harmondsworth, Middlesex, England

First published in the United States of America by Viking,
a division of Penguin Books USA Inc., 1995
Published in Puffin Books, 1996

1 3 5 7 9 10 8 6 4 2

THE LIBRARY OF CONGRESS HAS CATALOGED THE VIKING EDITION AS FOLLOWS:

Cooper, Ilene.
Stupid Cupid / by Ilene Cooper. p. cm. — (The Holiday Five)
Summary: Tired of her mother urging her to diet, twelve-year-old Maddy finds
the motivation to lose weight after meeting a handsome new student.
ISBN 0-670-85059-4
[1.Weight control—Fiction. 2. Mothers and daughters—Fiction.
3. Friendship—Fiction.]
I. Title. II. Series: Cooper, Ilene. Holiday Five
PZ7.C7856St 1995 [Fic]—dc20 94-38213 CIP AC

Puffin Books ISBN 0-14-036519-2

Printed in the United States of America

ONE

Maddy Donaldson sat at the kitchen table trying to read her history book, but it wasn't easy to concentrate. Every few minutes, she glanced over at the counter and the plate of freshly baked cookies a neighbor had brought.

"Your mother was so sweet to help me with those curtains." Mrs. Jesco beamed as she gave Maddy the treats. "I thought the least I could do was make her some of my special double chocolate chip cookies."

"They look great," Maddy told her.

"Well, have one, hon. I'm sure your mother won't mind."

Maddy nodded but thought to herself, That's what you think.

She had thanked Mrs. Jesco, put the plate on the

counter, and told herself sternly, "You are on a diet, Maddy. You've been on this diet since exactly eight o'clock this morning. Do yourself a favor, try to make it to at least eight o'clock tonight."

Feeling very virtuous, Maddy had sat back down and continued with the causes of the Civil War, but now all she was feeling was hungry, and all she could think about were those darn cookies. It was as if they were on the counter, calling, "Hey, Maddy, we're over here."

"I'll have a glass of milk," she decided. Milk was good for you, after all. Full of calcium and vitamins. If she had some milk, maybe she'd forget about the cookies.

Who was she kidding, she thought, after a couple of sips. Milk practically demanded cookies, especially chocolate chip cookies. The dark sweetness of the chocolate melted so nicely in the creaminess of the milk. Just thinking about it made her mouth water.

What difference could a couple of cookies make? Maddy reasoned. She'd make up for it at dinner. She'd skip the bread. Heck, she'd even skip the main course. Her mother had said they were going to have meat loaf. That shouldn't be too hard to give up. So, Maddy decided, it was all settled. She'd just have a salad and a few bites of the meat loaf, and then the cookies wouldn't even be a blip on her diet.

Deciding to take a break, Maddy brought the milk and the plate of cookies into the living room, where she could watch television while she had her snack. . . .

An hour later, she wasn't sure how it had happened. True, the talk show had been engrossing. It was about people who thought they had lived before. One woman was sure she had been Abraham Lincoln, which Maddy found particularly interesting, because her class was studying the Civil War. When the program ended, Maddy looked down at the plate of cookies and was shocked to see nothing on it but a pile of crumbs.

"Oh my gosh!" she exclaimed. Quickly, she took the plate and the empty glass to the kitchen, rinsed them out, and practically flung them into the dishwasher. She had to get rid of the evidence.

Glancing at the clock and seeing it was after five, Maddy knew she'd better start making the salad or her mother would be mad. As she scraped the carrots and chopped the mushrooms, Maddy was conscious of how tight her jeans felt.

Fifteen minutes later, Maddy heard her mother drive the car into the garage. She hoped Mrs. Jesco was nowhere around.

"Hi, Maddy," Mrs. Donaldson called from the hallway.

Maddy always liked it when her mother got home from her job as a paralegal at a law firm. It made the house seem warmer, more comforting. Maddy's father had died five years ago, when Maddy was seven. Maddy's grandfather, Paul Pappas, used to live with them, taking care of Maddy in the afternoon, but about a year ago he had decided to get his own apartment. He said he needed his privacy. At the time, Maddy had wondered what the heck an old guy like her grandfather needed privacy for. Then her grandfather brought the reason home: his lady friend, Alice.

"Oh, good, you're making the salad," Mrs. Donaldson said approvingly. "I'll just change clothes and start the meat loaf. Grandpa's going to join us for dinner."

"Where's Alice?" Maddy asked. Her grandfather and Alice dined together almost every evening.

"She's visiting her daughter in Milwaukee."

Maddy wasn't sure how she felt about Alice. She supposed it was nice for her grandfather to have someone to go bowling with or take to a movie. But it seemed weird to have a grandfather who was dating.

In a few minutes, Mrs. Donaldson had changed out of her suit and was downstairs in slacks and a sweater. She began preparing supper the way she did everything—efficiently. Maddy was just the opposite of her mother. She was a dreamer and never rushed. It drove her mom crazy.

"So," her mother said as she popped the frozen meat into the microwave to defrost, "how's the diet coming?"

"Fine," Maddy said grumpily. She wasn't going to confess that she had messed up so quickly. The whole stupid diet had been her mother's idea anyway. Maddy glanced over at her mother. Mrs. Donaldson was small and trim. Maddy was already taller than her mother, and she suspected she weighed more, as well. She concentrated on her chopping. She didn't want to think about that.

"You stuck to the plan?"

"I had yogurt and fruit for lunch." It wasn't a lie.

"That's good, honey. Maybe we should go for a walk after dinner for exercise."

"Mom, check your calendar. It's January."

"There's no law against taking walks in January," Mrs. Donaldson said mildly. "Besides, it's in the high thirties. That's not so cold."

"Cold enough. And you don't need to exercise," Maddy pointed out.

"I like to walk."

Well, of course. And in the summer her mother liked

to bike-ride. She also took aerobics classes. Maddy could get tired just thinking about it.

"We'll see," Maddy finally said, pleased that she had come up with that particular phrase. After all, it was what her mother always said when she wasn't sure about giving in on some particular request.

An hour later the meat loaf was done, and Maddy had to admit it smelled pretty good. She was setting the table when her grandfather walked in, not bothering to knock.

"Hello, hello," he called.

"Hi, Grandpa," Maddy replied, coming out to the hall to give him a kiss. He was big and rumpled and smelled like pipe tobacco.

"How's my pumpkin?"

Maddy wrinkled her nose. She had told her grandfather not to call her that anymore. It had been all right when she was little, but she didn't think it was a proper nickname for a seventh grader. Besides, she had been cute when she was little. Now, she really was as round as a pumpkin.

"I'm okay," she said with a sigh. No point in arguing with him now. Besides, he'd probably still be calling her Pumpkin on the day she walked down the aisle. If that should ever happen.

They walked into the kitchen.

"Hi, Dad," Mrs. Donaldson greeted her father. "Is it getting colder outside?"

"Not too bad," Mr. Pappas responded, sitting down at the table and taking a piece of rye bread from the bread basket.

"Dad, you're going to ruin your supper."

"Not me. I've been waiting all day for your meat loaf."

"Well, here it is," Mrs. Donaldson said, putting it on the table next to the mashed potatoes.

Maddy hadn't known her mother had made mashed potatoes. They were her favorite.

As her mother and grandfather talked about what had happened that day at the law firm, Maddy tried to decide what to put on her plate. She vaguely remembered her plan about salad and a little bit of meat loaf, but her hearty appetite had once again reappeared. The cookies and milk seemed a long time ago.

Her mother noticed she hadn't taken any food. "I think you can have a little bit of everything." She turned to her father. "Maddy's on a diet."

"Again?" Mr. Pappas snorted.

"Dad!"

"Foolishness. Maddy's only a girl. She'll lose her baby fat in time."

Maddy felt torn by her grandfather's comment. She was glad he thought dieting was a waste of time. At this moment, with all that good-looking food on the table, she agreed totally. But baby fat? That sounded disgusting.

"Just a little bit of everything," her mother repeated, looking steadily at Maddy. "And more than a little bit of the salad."

Maddy helped herself to a nice, large portion of the salad, a slice of the meat loaf, and a spoonful of the potatoes. When her mother left the table to get some water, she added a dollop of butter to the potatoes.

Before the other two diners were even half done, Maddy's plate was clean.

"You're finished?" her mother noticed, startled.

"I was hungry."

"Well," Mrs. Donaldson continued uncertainly, "I guess if all you had for lunch was fruit and yogurt, you can have a little more."

"Thanks, Mom," Maddy said happily. She took another piece of meat loaf and more mashed potatoes. Content with her food, she tuned in on the dinner conversation.

"Did you read about Mr. Gray in the paper?" Mrs. Donaldson was asking her father.

Grandpa nodded. "He's one smart guy. He's going to

get to the bottom of that land development deal. He's got the mayor on the run."

Mrs. Donaldson, her eyes bright, agreed. "It's such a pleasure to work with him. He's smart and really good about advising the younger lawyers. If I ever decide to go back to law school, I'll really have an advantage having worked for him. And he's such a nice man."

"Sounds like you have a crush on him," Grandpa teased.

"Oh, Dad, get serious. I'm a little old for a crush, don't you think?"

What did her mother think about men? Maddy wondered, as she finished up her second helping of potatoes. Her mother had dated now and again over the years, but never very seriously nor for very long. She spent her days going to work and her evenings taking care of Maddy. Maddy had never thought about it much, but on reflection, it seemed like kind of a boring life. Maybe she wasn't quite comfortable with her grandfather having a girlfriend, but she was sure that he had lots more fun than her mother.

Grandpa must have been thinking the same thing. Putting down his napkin, he said, "You should be picking out someone, Patricia. Don't you think it's about time?"

"Picking out someone? Dad, it's not like going to the grocery store and finding the right cantaloupe."

That made Maddy giggle, but she turned the laugh into a cough when her mother gave her a look.

Grandpa shrugged. "Sorry. It's funny, though, I'm the only one dating in this family."

"Maddy is too young to date," Mrs. Donaldson said firmly. "And I'm not interested in dating."

"That's not natural, Patricia."

"Dad . . ." Maddy's mother said warningly.

Throwing down his napkin, Grandpa said, "All right, I'll butt out."

"Thank you." Mrs. Donaldson got up and cleared the table. "Do you want coffee?"

"Sure. What's for dessert?"

"I can give you some frozen yogurt, but I'm not baking as long as Maddy's on her diet."

"What about those cookies Mrs. Jesco sent over?" Grandpa asked innocently. "Can we bring those out?"

Darn, Maddy thought. Double darn.

"What cookies?" Mrs. Donaldson asked.

"I saw Mrs. Jesco on the way in. She said to be sure and have some of the double chocolate chippers she sent over."

Mrs. Donaldson looked inquiringly at Maddy, who

tried to disappear into her chair—not an easy feat after all she had eaten.

Her mother's look of puzzlement turned to a frown. "Maddy, where are the cookies?"

Maddy wished desperately she had a dog to blame for the lack of cookies, but her mother wouldn't even let her have a bird.

"Well . . ." She couldn't think of anything else to say, and the silence lasted until her mother figured it all out without Maddy's help.

"Oh, Maddy."

Just those two words, said in that disappointed tone of voice, made Maddy feel worse than if her mom had yelled at her.

"I'm sorry," Maddy said, her eyes starting to water.

Mrs. Donaldson turned away and began to make the coffee. "Never mind. It doesn't matter."

Grandpa was a little slower, but finally he, too, puzzled it out. He turned his piercing blue eyes in her direction. "You ate the cookies, Maddy? Every last one of them?"

Maddy nodded.

"Well, they must have been good."

That made Maddy smile a little. But the worst thing was, she knew she would have eaten them even if they hadn't been all that good. She got up and went over to her mother. "I'll do better tomorrow. I'll try harder."

Mrs. Donaldson patted her on the shoulder. "I know."

"I didn't even know I had eaten the whole plateful."

Grandpa cleared his throat. "Patricia, who wants this diet, you or Maddy?"

Bringing the coffee over, Mrs. Donaldson said, "What do you mean?"

"Well, who wants the weight off Maddy, you or her?"

"I'm sure Maddy would like to be thinner."

Grandpa turned to Maddy. "That true?"

"Well, yeah, of course." Plenty of times she wished she was thinner. Just never when she was eating.

"Are you willing to be on a diet to knock off the pounds?"

"I don't seem to be able to stick to a diet," she responded quietly.

Grandpa took a sip of his coffee. "Maddy has to want to diet, Patricia. You can decorate the house with carrot sticks, but you can't watch every bite she eats."

Mrs. Donaldson looked at Maddy sadly. "I guess not."

Maddy didn't think she could take any more of her mother's disappointment. She began to get angry. "I'm not that heavy, Mom. You make it seem like I should go off to be the fat lady in the circus."

"I do not," her mother protested.

"I happen to be big boned, like Daddy." Unlike you, she added silently, angrily.

"You are built like your father," Mrs. Donaldson agreed, trying to calm the situation.

But Maddy was just getting started. "You just want me to be like you, but you're not so perfect."

Mrs. Donaldson flushed. "I never said—I don't know how this got to be about me."

Slapping his hand on the table, Grandpa said, "That's enough. Does anyone want my opinion?"

Both Maddy and her mother looked as if they'd like to say no, but they both knew there was no stopping Paul Pappas when he had something to say.

Taking their silence for agreement, he continued. "Maddy, your mother is trying to help you. Don't make her into a bad guy. Patricia, Maddy is going to start losing weight when she has a reason to lose weight. You can't make her."

"All right, all right," Mrs. Donaldson said wearily. "I knew that. I can't help it if I worry about Maddy."

Maddy sighed. She had the feeling she'd do a whole lot better with diets—and everything else—if her mother didn't worry quite so much.

Two

"I heard Abraham Lincoln was psychic." Maddy looked over at her friend Jeanne. "Right before he died he dreamed he saw himself in a casket."

Jeanne frowned. "I don't think that's going to be on the test."

The girls were studying together for their Civil War test tomorrow. Jeanne was sitting at the desk in Maddy's bedroom, looking over their history book and picking out questions to ask. Maddy was on the bed trying to stay awake.

"I know that, Jeanne," Maddy said a little irritably. Jeanne was her best friend, but she was just the opposite of Maddy in practically everything. Japanese American, Jeanne was short, thin, and had black hair that hung perfectly to her shoulders. She was passionate about her schoolwork and serious most of the time, though she could display a wicked sense of humor. "It's just more interesting to think about Lincoln being psychic than about the Battle of Gettysburg."

Jeanne closed the book. "Maybe we should take a break. Do you want to go downstairs and get some Cokes and potato chips?"

"I guess," Maddy said a little hesitantly. Since the cookie episode, she had been trying to watch what she ate. She wasn't exactly on a diet, but she wanted to make sure she didn't down a bag of potato chips without noticing.

The girls went downstairs. Mrs. Donaldson was in the small den watching television. "We're going to get something to eat," Maddy said as she walked by. Her mother just nodded.

Maddy poured the Coke and put the chips in a bowl. When they were settled, Jeanne said, "Does your mom ever get lonely?"

"What do you mean?"

"I don't know, it seems like she's always in the den by herself watching TV."

"Well, usually, I'm with her."

"Still . . ."

"I know. I've been thinking lately she should get out more, too," Maddy admitted.

"She's really nice looking. I should think she could have dates. Isn't there anyone she's interested in?"

"There is this one guy. His name is Mr. Gray. He works with my mom at the law firm. She talks about him all the time."

Jeanne looked intrigued. "Has he ever asked her out?"

Maddy shook her head.

"Maybe he's married."

"No, he's divorced."

"They why doesn't he ask her out?"

"I don't know, Jeanne."

Jeanne sipped her cola thoughtfully. "They probably would like to get together, but they're too shy."

"Adults don't get shy," Maddy scoffed. "Not like that."

"They do, too. My aunt Kyoko was so shy she didn't date at all until she was thirty. Then she went to see a shrink about it and she wound up marrying him."

"I don't think my mother has any plans to go into therapy," Maddy said.

Jeanne leaned forward. "Maybe there's something we could do about getting her and this Mr. Gray together."

"Yeah, right," Maddy responded skeptically.

But Jeanne was off and running. "We could go to her office and tell this man your mom likes him."

"My mother would kill me," Maddy said adamantly.

"Not if he liked her too and they got together. She'd be forever grateful."

"I wouldn't have the nerve."

Jeanne smiled. "I would."

That was another way the girls were different. Maddy was a 'fraidy cat. Nothing scared Jeanne.

"I'll think about it," Maddy said. She'd think about it for so long that Jeanne would forget about it. Maddy decided she'd better change the subject. "My friend Lia is coming over on Saturday. Do you want to hang out with us?"

"Lia, your friend from camp?"

Maddy nodded. She had made four very good friends at camp: Lia, Kathy, Erin, and Jill. When camp ended, they had vowed to get together during the school year, so they had formed a sort of club, the Holiday Five. They met around holidays, like Halloween and New Year's, but sometimes they got together individually, too.

"I wish I could," Jeanne said regretfully, "but we're going into Chicago on Saturday to visit my grandmother."

"Well, maybe next time. I'd like you to meet my camp friends."

Mrs. Donaldson walked into the kitchen. Though it probably wasn't obvious to Jeanne, Maddy noticed that the first thing her mother did was check out the amount of food on the table. Maddy could feel herself starting to get mad. Why didn't her mother just hide a video camera in the kitchen so that every time Maddy snuck into the fridge, she could get it on tape?

"Are you girls doing okay?" Mrs. Donaldson asked pleasantly.

"We're fine," Jeanne replied.

"How's the studying going?"

"Would you like me to name the five main reasons for the Civil War?" Maddy asked.

"Tell me later," Mrs. Donaldson said. She glanced at the now almost empty bag of chips. "You should have made some popcorn. It has fewer calories."

Since Jeanne was as slim as a flower, it was obvious who Mrs. Donaldson was talking to. Maddy cringed.

Her mother noticed her embarrassment and said, "Well, it doesn't really matter. Better get back to your studying, girls. Your father will be here to pick you up in a little while, Jeanne."

Later, after Maddy had gotten into her pajamas and climbed into bed, she remembered what Jeanne had said about her mother and Mr. Gray. Maybe if her mom had something to think about, something like a boyfriend, she wouldn't be so interested in every bite that Maddy put into her mouth. It might not hurt to go check out this Mr. Gray, Maddy decided as she drifted off to sleep. It might not hurt at all.

The next morning, Maddy could feel her stomach twitching as she walked into her classroom. The history test was going to be first period, and even though Maddy had gotten up early to study, she still didn't feel prepared. Maddy had a thing about tests. No matter how much she studied, she always got nervous during the test, and by the time she handed in her test paper, she was sure she had screwed up. Sometimes she surprised herself and did better than she expected. But often she got answers wrong that she should have gotten right.

"Where's Mrs. Dodge?" Maddy asked Jeanne, who sat in front of her, as she slid into her seat. The bell was ringing. Usually, you could set your watch by Mrs. Dodge.

"Maybe she's sick," Jeanne said happily.

"A substitute would be great," Maddy agreed.

But after a few moments, Mrs. Dodge walked into the room, accompanied by a boy. And not just any boy.

This was one of the best-looking boys Maddy had ever seen. He was tall with black hair that kept falling into his eyes. He wore a leather jacket over his flannel shirt, and Maddy wondered if that was the coat he had worn to school. If it was, he had probably frozen on the way. It had dipped into the twenties this morning.

"Class, this is Mickey Torres," Mrs. Dodge said. "He will be joining us for the rest of the semester." Mrs. Dodge made it sound as if he had been asked to join a select club, rather than just being assigned to room 301.

She turned to Mickey. "We're having a test on the Civil War this morning. Do you feel lucky?"

Mickey looked confused. Maddy immediately felt sorry for him. It had taken the class half the semester to get used to Mrs. Dodge's sense of humor.

"Oh, I'm just kidding," Mrs. Dodge said. "We'll give you a break today."

"Good," Mickey muttered.

Mrs. Dodge glanced around the class. "We have a free seat next to Maddy. Maddy, raise your hand."

Flushing a little, Maddy timidly raised her hand. She didn't know if she liked being singled out for Mickey.

But Mickey didn't pay any attention to her. He just slid into his seat and looked down at his desk.

As Mrs. Dodge passed out the test, Maddy snuck a look at Mickey. He was tapping his fingers on his knees. He had long, slim hands, she noticed.

Concentrate, Maddy told herself. On the test, not on the new kid.

She was relieved to see that much of the test was multiple choice. At least she'd have a fighting chance with those questions. The fill-in-the-blanks she'd worry about later.

When it was finally over, Maddy thought she had done all right on the test. "Was it hard?" Mickey leaned over and whispered as the papers were being collected.

Startled to hear his voice, Maddy couldn't find hers, so she just shook her head. Then she cursed herself for not being quick enough to come up with a witty rejoinder.

At lunch, all the girls were talking about the new boy.

"He's cute," Denise Jenkins said as she daintily ate one of her cut-up carrots. Maddy couldn't figure out how she survived on all that rabbit food she ate.

"He looks older than the other boys," Jeanne said.

"That's because he's tall, not a midget like most of them," Sarah Sanderson replied.

Mickey was taller than Maddy, she'd noticed that

right away, and that was reason enough for her to like him. With most of the other boys, she felt like Goliath.

As the bell rang signaling that lunch was over, Maddy leaned over to Jeanne. "I've been thinking about what you said last night."

Jeanne looked blank.

"About my mom."

"Oh, that she should get a boyfriend?"

The girls walked out of the lunchroom. "Not just that. About Mr. Gray. I think we should go down to the law firm and check him out."

Jeanne looked intrigued. "And then what?"

Maddy hadn't really thought that far ahead, but she improvised. "Maybe we could talk to him about my mom."

"We'd have to be subtle," Jeanne warned.

Maddy wasn't even sure she knew what subtle meant.

Jeanne must have figured that out because she said, "You know, low-key. We can't just go in there and tell Mr. Gray he should be dating your mom. You were right, she would kill us."

"So then what?"

Jeanne thought for a moment. "If we get the chance, we should just talk about what a nice person your mother is. What a good mom."

Maddy guessed she was a good mom. Most of the time.

"Then maybe he'll get the idea on his own," Jeanne continued.

"Can we go after school?" Maddy asked. She wanted to get this started before she lost her nerve.

"Sure. I just have to call my mom and tell her I'm going downtown."

"I think my mother said she was going to be at the library all day doing research, so she won't even be around."

"Perfect." Jeanne smiled.

At precisely three-thirty, Maddy and Jeanne walked into the law offices of Hustings, Walters, and Gray. Maddy went up to the receptionist's desk and said, "Hi, I'm Mrs. Donaldson's daughter. Is she here?"

The girls had decided on the bus that if Maddy's mother was in the office, they'd pretend they were just coming to say hello on their way to the library.

"Sorry, she's not here right now. So you're her daughter?"

Maddy nodded.

"She talks about you all the time."

Maddy wasn't sure if she liked that or not. "Is it okay if we wait in her office?"

The receptionist hesitated for a moment. Then she

said, "I guess it will be all right. Do you know where it is?"

"Down the hall and to the right?"

The receptionist nodded absently as she answered the ringing phone.

"Now what?" Maddy whispered to Jeanne.

"Let's look for Mr. Gray's office. It probably has his name on the door."

Maddy was glad that Jeanne was with her. There was no way she'd be able to pull this off by herself.

They walked down a long hall, passing Mrs. Donaldson's cubbyhole of an office. Maddy peeked in and saw a picture of herself on her mother's desk.

"Hey," Jeanne hissed. "Over here."

Maddy hurried down the hall. Jeanne was standing beside a heavy oak door with the name *William Gray* next to it. The door was shut.

"Now what?" Maddy repeated.

Even Jeanne looked stymied. Just then, the door swung open, and a handsome man in an expensive-looking suit looked at them with a surprised expression.

"Hello," he said. "Are you waiting for me?"

Maddy and Jeanne exchanged looks. "No," Jeanne finally responded. "We were just . . . looking around."

"Oh," the man answered with amusement. "Well, I'm afraid there isn't much to see around here."

Maddy couldn't take her eyes off the man. She had expected Mr. Gray to be nice looking, but this man was almost movie-star handsome. What a day—first Mickey Torres, now William Gray. It was like she was in Hollywood or something.

"Her mother works here," Jeanne said, nodding at Maddy.

"Who's that?" Mr. Gray turned his gaze on Maddy.

"Ah . . . Patricia Donaldson."

"Really." Mr. Gray seemed a bit surprised at that. Maddy wondered if it was because they looked so little alike. "Well, you should be very proud of your mother. She's a very good worker. The best paralegal we've ever had."

Maddy didn't know if thank you was the appropriate response, but she said it anyway.

Mr. Gray moved as if to walk past them, but Jeanne stepped forward. "Mrs. Donaldson's a widow, you know."

Maddy stared at Jeanne in horror. How obvious could you get?

"Yes, I know. I'm sorry about your dad," he said to Maddy.

"That's probably why she works so hard," Jeanne continued. "Because she has to take care of Maddy and all."

A slight smile crossed Mr. Gray's lips. "Sounds like you think Mrs. Donaldson should get a raise."

Maddy closed her eyes. He thought she and Jeanne were here to hit him up for a raise. If her mother ever found out about this, she was dead meat.

"Well, maybe I should take that up with Mr. Gray."

Maddy's eyes flew open. "Aren't you Mr. Gray?"

The man laughed. "Hardly. I'm David Ebersoll. I'm just a junior partner."

"But you were coming out of Mr. Gray's office," Jeanne squeaked.

"Just dropping off a file."

"Oh," Jeanne said in a small voice.

"But here's Mr. Gray if you'd like to meet him."

The girls followed David Ebersoll's gaze. Coming down the hall was a tiny little man with silver hair, leaning heavily on a cane. Maddy wasn't sure how old he was, but he was older than her grandfather.

"We don't want to meet him," Maddy said. She could feel her face redden.

"No. Bye," Jeanne said. "Nice talking to you."

Maddy and Jeanne almost crashed into each other in their hurry to escape.

They had to walk right by Mr. Gray to get back to Maddy's mom's office, but they just nodded when he looked at them curiously. Once they had closed the door to the office, they burst into nervous giggles.

"You don't think that Mr. Ebersoll will tell, do you?" Maddy asked when she had caught her breath enough to talk.

"You'll have to tell her we were here," Jeanne responded. "He probably will mention that."

"Why do I have to tell?" Maddy asked. "It was your idea."

"She's your mom."

Maddy couldn't argue with that. "Let's get out of here," Maddy said. "I'll tell her at dinner. But from now on my mother can just figure out her own love life."

Jeanne looked disappointed. "Just because Mr. Gray was a little older than her . . ."

"A little!"

"Okay, so a lot. It doesn't mean we have to give up," Jeanne said.

Maddy shook her head. She didn't even want to think about the trouble they could have gotten into. "Forget it, Jeanne. My days as a matchmaker are over."

Three

At dinner, Maddy casually told her mother about going to her office. Mrs. Donaldson wasn't angry about the girls' visit. But she was surprised.

"Maddy, I've asked you to come down to the office lots of times, and you never wanted to. I think you've been there exactly twice since I started working there."

"Well, it just seemed like a good idea," Maddy replied vaguely. She pushed the spaghetti around on her plate. For once, she wasn't hungry.

"I can't imagine what got into you. I hope you were polite to Mr. Ebersoll."

"Yeah, we were. He said you were a really hard worker."

"That was nice of him. I wish he'd tell Mr. Gray that, so I could get a raise."

Maddy looked at her mother suspiciously, but Mrs. Donaldson was innocently eating her dinner. Apparently, Mr. Ebersoll hadn't mentioned that very suggestion, nor the girls mistaking him for Mr. Gray.

"How long did you stay?" her mother asked conversationally.

"Not long."

"Did you meet anyone else?"

"Well," Maddy said hesitantly, "we saw Mr. Gray."

"Did Dave introduce you?"

"No, he just pointed him out. I didn't know he was so old," Maddy said.

Mrs. Donaldson, who was ignoring her spaghetti and concentrating on her salad, said, "He's only in his late sixties."

Maddy rolled her eyes. *Only?*

"So what do you have planned for the weekend?" Mrs. Donaldson asked.

"Don't you remember?" Maddy asked anxiously. "Lia's coming tomorrow."

"That's right," Mrs. Donaldson said. "Is she taking the train up?"

Maddy nodded. "We have to pick her up at the station. She's coming on the noon train."

Mrs. Donaldson smiled. "I'm glad you're keeping in touch with your camp friends."

"They're the best," Maddy said. Maddy adored Jeanne and she had other friends at school, but the Holiday Five had formed a special bond. The girls all lived in Chicago suburbs, except for Erin, who lived in the city. The commuter train had stations in all of their suburbs, which made it easy for them to get together.

Maddy and her mother were running a little late the next day, but they got to the station just as the train was pulling in. Lia was the first one off. She came running up to them and gave Maddy a hug.

"Lia, this is my mother," Maddy said, once she had disengaged herself.

"Hello, Lia. It's nice to finally meet you."

Lia gave Mrs. Donaldson a big smile. "Nice to meet you, too."

As they walked to the car, Mrs. Donaldson said, "I'm going to the gym for a while. Do you girls want to stay downtown and have something to eat?"

"I'm starved," Lia said.

"We'll go to the Burger Shack," Maddy said. "Everything there is good, the hamburgers, the fries, the shakes . . ." Maddy's voice trailed off as she saw her mother looking at her. Well, lunch is ruined, she thought. She wouldn't be able to choke down a bag of fries without a vision of her mother standing over her, the same pained expression on her face.

But Mrs. Donaldson didn't say anything about food. She just drove them over to the Burger Shack and told them to have a good time. "Call me if you want a ride home."

"We can walk," Maddy replied.

"It's awfully cold," Mrs. Donaldson said. "I'll be home in an hour or so."

"Your mother is nice," Lia said as they found their way to a booth. She took off her jacket and shook her blond braid loose from her hat. "You don't look very much like her."

Maddy stiffened. "I look like my father."

But Lia didn't realize she had made a faux pas. She just said, "You must miss him."

"I do." Maddy did miss her father, but not all the time. Sometimes she forgot about him for weeks at a time, and then when he did pop into her mind, she felt terribly guilty. Sometimes, though, she'd hear a snatch of song he used to sing to her or see a man on the street who resembled him, and a wave of longing would wash over her so strong that it brought tears to her eyes.

Maddy picked up the menu. She didn't want to talk about her father. "The hamburgers here are really great—oh, I told you that."

"I'm going to have a cheeseburger and some fries.

Will you split the fries with me? I don't want to eat them all."

Lia didn't have a weight problem, probably because she never ate all her fries. But Maddy gratefully accepted her offer of sharing. Feeling virtuous, she ordered a diet cola to drink.

"So, what's new?" Lia asked after the waitress had left with their order. "What have you been doing for fun?"

Maddy made a face. "Nothing. It's been too cold for fun." Then she brightened. "But my mother did say I could take horseback riding lessons in the spring." Maddy loved horses. She had done as much riding as she could at camp, and now with lessons, she hoped she could get really good.

"That's great," Lia said. "My parents want me to take piano lessons." She made a face.

"It would be neat to play an instrument," Maddy argued.

"I'd rather learn guitar, but my dad says if I do well with the piano, then I can move on to the guitar."

Maddy shook her head. "Why do parents always think what they want you to do is such a great idea?"

"And what you want to do isn't a great idea," Lia added.

As they ate their lunch, with Maddy being careful not to take more than her share of the french fries, the girls chattered about school, clothes, and their Holiday Five friends.

"How's Scott?" Maddy asked.

Scott was Lia's next-door neighbor. Although they were just good friends, there had been a rumor around school that they were much more. When the Holiday Five had come to Lia's for Halloween, there had been so many fireworks, it seemed more like the Fourth of July.

"He's fine. Everything's back to normal," Lia said. "There's just one problem."

"What's that?"

"I'm beginning to think maybe I do like him more than just a friend."

"You're kidding! After all that fuss you made?"

Lia gave an embarrassed shrug. "He's getting cuter every day."

"He was pretty cute," Maddy agreed. "A really cute guy started at my school the other day, and the teacher sat him right next to me. His name is Mickey Torres."

"What does he look like?" Lia asked with interest.

Maddy had just begun describing Mickey when she

caught sight of someone ordering at the take-out counter. "Ohmigosh."

"What?" Lia swiveled her head in the direction Maddy was looking.

"There he is," Maddy hissed.

Sure enough, there was Mickey, still in his leather jacket, though with a long purple scarf wrapped around his neck, placing his order.

"Ooh, he's adorable," Lia whispered.

"Don't look," Maddy replied, pretending to fiddle with her napkin. The last thing she wanted was for Mickey to turn around and see them staring.

Lia immediately turned back toward Maddy. "Have you talked to him?"

"A little. He's asked me a couple of questions about assignments and stuff." Maddy didn't add that every time Mickey had leaned over to borrow a pencil or ask what page they were on, her heart had fluttered just a bit faster.

"Well, maybe we should go over and say hello. We've finished eating. We could just go up and pay the bill, kind of casual-like and then . . ."

Maddy shook her head. "I don't think so."

Lia shrugged. "Okay."

"I wonder where he's going?" Maddy said.

"We could follow him," Lia said, finishing off the last of the french fries.

Maddy looked startled. "You're kidding."

"What's the big deal? After he gets his food, we'll just casually walk a block or so behind him. Maybe we can find out where he lives."

Maddy wondered why all her friends had to have such big, brave ideas. Still, the prospect of finding out a little more about Mickey Torres was enticing.

"What if he sees us?"

"He won't," Lia said confidently.

"Well, maybe we could follow him for just a block or two," Maddy consented.

The girls counted out the money for the check and tip, and they had enough just to leave it on the table without having to stand in line waiting for the cashier. They waited until Mickey had gotten his food and slammed the door behind him, and then hurriedly put on their coats and walked outside.

It had gotten colder. Heavy, gray clouds made it seem as if it were almost evening, rather than early afternoon.

"Boy, we picked a great day to be the Hardy Boys," Maddy grumbled, zipping her down jacket. She fumbled in her pocket for earmuffs.

"Nancy Drew," Lia corrected. "Do you see him?"

"There he is," Maddy said, "down by the bank."

Keeping a discreet distance, the girls followed Mickey as he walked past the downtown shopping center into a block of rundown houses. He was eating something out of his bag and sipping a drink. When he stopped at one of the houses, the girls slowed down and waited until he walked inside.

"I wonder if he lives there?" Lia said.

"It isn't very nice," Maddy noted. The house needed painting badly and there was a rusty old bike on the front lawn.

"Maybe we had better just keep walking," Lia said. "We don't know how long he's going to be in there."

But the words were barely out of her mouth when Mickey walked out, holding a little girl by the hand.

The girls were practically in front of the house.

"He's going to see us," Maddy gasped.

Sure enough, as he exited the yard, Mickey looked over in their direction and caught Maddy's eye. He gave the girls a small wave, but his brow was furrowed, as if he wasn't quite sure who Maddy was.

"We better say hi," Lia whispered.

Slowly, they walked over. *Just let him remember my name,* Maddy prayed. It would be so humiliating if he didn't.

The little girl, all bundled up in a pink ski jacket and pink hat with bunnies on it, was jumping up and down. "Who are you?" she chirped.

Maddy could have hugged her. "I'm Maddy. I go to school with Mickey. This is my friend Lia."

"I'm Linda. Mickey's my brother. We're going to the park. Do you want to come?"

Mickey laughed. "We can't shut her up sometimes."

"She's adorable," Lia said sincerely.

"I'm four," Linda informed her. Then she looked up at Mickey. "It's cold. Let's go to the park."

"Do you want to come?" he asked, looking at Lia. "It would be more fun. For both of us."

Lia turned to Maddy, who tried to look as if she didn't care one way or the other. "I guess we've got some time."

"Good. I was kind of dreading this, but I promised."

The park wasn't very far away. Snow was beginning to fall, but that didn't deter Linda, who wanted to be pushed on the swings.

Maddy and Lia sat on one of the benches and watched while Mickey gave Linda a few solid pushes.

"You're right," Lia told Maddy. "He really is cute."

"He'll probably have a girlfriend soon," Maddy said, a little sadly.

Mickey walked over to the girls. "Linda wants to

swing by herself now. Good thing, too. She's little, but she can wear you out."

Maddy was tongue-tied, but Lia said, "You're a good brother."

To Maddy's amazement, Mickey reddened, but maybe it was just from the cold.

"Well, my mom, she's sick a lot, so I take care of Linda."

"Where's your dad?" Lia asked.

Maddy's eyes darted over to Mickey. She hated it when people asked her that question. But all Mickey did was shrug. "He left a couple of years ago."

"So how do you like Waukegan?" Maddy said, trying to change the subject.

Mickey turned his attention to her. "It's okay."

"Do you like school?"

"School's school. But in this one, I'm about a million miles behind."

"Maddy could probably help you catch up," Lia said boldly.

Maddy wanted to die, and Mickey looked uncomfortable.

"She's really good in math," Lia continued.

What was Lia talking about? Maddy thought. Math was her best subject, but she wasn't all *that* good in it.

"Really?" Now Mickey looked interested. "I wasn't too good at math at my last school. And here they're doing all that algebra stuff."

"Pre-algebra," Maddy corrected.

"Great," Mickey groaned. "If this is only the 'pre' part, I'm gonna get killed when it comes time for the real thing."

"That won't happen this year," Maddy said.

Mickey didn't look comforted. "Maybe we could go over our homework sometime."

Maddy wanted to shout, "Yes! Yes! Name the day!" But she knew enough to be casual. "Sure, whenever." She was very proud of that *whenever.*

The three of them talked about school for a few minutes more until Linda came rushing over.

"It's cold," she declared, as if she had just realized it.

All three of them laughed.

"Does that mean you want to go home?" Mickey asked.

Linda nodded. "Can we build a snowman when we get there?"

"Linda, there's not enough snow yet," her brother told her.

"There will be," she said confidently.

"All right," Mickey said. "When there's enough

snow, we will." Mickey got up. "Let's go home. We'll have hot chocolate."

Linda turned to the girls. "Are you coming too?"

"Oh, I don't think they want to," Mickey interjected.

Maddy was about to say, "Oh yes we do," but Lia answered first. "I don't think we can, Linda. Not today."

"Well, maybe some other time," Mickey said, obviously relieved. "Come on, Linda, let's go."

As soon as they were out of earshot, Maddy turned to Lia. "Why didn't you want to go?"

"I didn't think Mickey really wanted us. If his mom is sick, he doesn't need us barging in."

"Oh, I didn't think of that," Maddy said, embarrassed that she hadn't. All she had been able to think of was how much she liked being with Mickey.

FOUR

For once in her life, Maddy wasn't hungry.

Her mother had gone to a lot of trouble to make fried chicken, but Maddy just nibbled at a chicken leg.

"Are you not feeling well?" Mrs. Donaldson said, looking at Maddy with concern.

"Uh . . . no. I'm fine."

"Maybe you're catching a cold," Lia offered.

"I'm all right," Maddy said impatiently. She just couldn't keep her mind off Mickey, that was all.

When they got home from the park, Lia and Maddy had settled down in the den to hash over every minute of the meeting. Lia was supposed to take the five o'clock train home, but they had been so deep in conversation, they'd forgotten to wake Mrs. Donaldson from her nap so she could get Lia to the train station.

After a hurried conversation with both mothers, it was decided that Lia could stay for supper, and Maddy and her mother would drive her home afterward.

And now, even though Maddy had discussed Mickey down to the color of his socks, he still wasn't out of her brain. How could she think about food, when she was so busy thinking about him?

Still, it wasn't polite just to let her mother make conversation with Lia. And she didn't want her mother to get suspicious, either. The last thing Maddy wanted was to have her mom start prying into her thoughts.

You can think about him later, she told herself. Tonight, when she was in bed with the lights off. Then she could go over it all again.

Turning back to Lia and her mother, Maddy said, "How was your day, Mom?"

Mrs. Donaldson laughed. "Now I know you're not feeling well. I don't think you've ever asked me that, Maddy."

Maddy was offended. "Sorry. I just thought it would be polite."

"It was," Mrs. Donaldson said soothingly. "Just unexpected. Well, let's see. After I dropped you off, I went to the gym, and then I stopped at the library. I came home and took a nap, and then I made dinner. Pretty exciting, huh?"

After dinner, when Maddy and Lia were clearing the table, Lia said, "Does your mother date much?"

"Funny you should ask," Maddy responded. She told Lia all about how she and Jeanne went down to the law office to check out Mr. Gray. "And boy, he really was gray," Maddy finished. "A guy in his sixties."

Lia shook her head. "That's too bad. But it shouldn't be too hard for her to find someone. You mom is really cute."

"You'd think she might find someone at the gym," Maddy said, as she shoved the leftover chicken into the refrigerator, "but she's been going there for a long time, and she's never mentioned anyone. I wonder how a person goes about getting her mom fixed up."

Lia looked thoughtful. "I know someone she could get fixed up with."

"Who?" Maddy asked, startled.

"My uncle Danny."

Maddy stopped cleaning up and sat down at the table. "Tell me about him."

Lia kept rinsing dishes. "Well, he's very nice. And funny. He's got curly hair and gray eyes. He's my mom's baby brother."

"Baby brother?" Maddy frowned. She had visions of a man walking around in diapers. "How old is he?"

"That's what my mom calls him," Lia said placatingly. "Let's see, I guess he's in his middle thirties somewhere."

"My mother is thirty-six."

Lia put down her towel. "Just about right."

"This is great," Maddy said, feeling her enthusiasm growing. "I think we should do something about it."

"Me too," Lia agreed.

"Why, if they got married we'd be..." Maddy thought about it for a second. "Cousins, kind of."

Before they could delve into the new world of kinship, Mrs. Donaldson came into the kitchen. Maddy suddenly felt a little protective of her mother. She didn't know what fate had in store for her.

"I think we'd better get going, Lia. I don't want to get you back too late."

While they were putting on their coats, Lia whispered, "I'll call you this week. We can figure out the details."

Maddy nodded. She wondered if she would be her mother's maid of honor.

"Boy," Jeanne said, "I go away for one weekend, and when I come back, you've got a new life."

The girls were whispering across the lunch table in the cafeteria. Maddy had been trying to fill Jeanne in on spending time with Mickey, but it wasn't easy, since they hadn't had a moment alone. This information was for Jeanne's ears only. Maddy didn't want Denise and the others knowing that she had spent time with Mickey. They'd just tease.

"Let's get out of here," Maddy said. "We can go to the library and talk."

Jeanne nodded. They gathered up the remains of their lunches and threw them in the wastebasket after muttering to the other girls that they needed to check some books out of the library.

Miss Drake, the librarian, waved at the girls when they came in. She was a live-and-let-live librarian. As long as the students weren't hurling books across the room or laughing like a pack of hyenas, she pretty much allowed them to go about their business. For Maddy and Jeanne, this meant finding a quiet corner of the library where they were unlikely to be disturbed.

They found it at a table behind the stacks. "Now, let me get this straight," Jeanne said. "You spent the afternoon with Mickey Torres, and he was really nice, and now you think he might like you?"

Maddy winced. Hearing Jeanne say it like that, well, it sounded dumb. Just because Mickey was nice to her didn't mean he liked her as a girlfriend. She knew that. Before anything like boyfriend-girlfriend stuff could happen, she'd probably have to lose some weight. But if there was even a chance Mickey would like her, she could diet off those pounds if she set her mind to it. She had already started to cut down on her eating.

"I don't think he likes me," Maddy said slowly. "I mean, not right now."

"What do you mean?"

"Maybe if I lost some weight . . ." This was so embarrassing.

But Jeanne was encouraging. "This is good," she said. "Going on a diet is good. Why, Maddy, you'd be so pretty if you lost weight."

"Now you sound like my mother," Maddy muttered.

"I know you don't like to talk about this—"

"I sure don't."

Even with her closest friends, Maddy hated to talk about dieting. Most of them studiously ignored the topic, except for Erin. Of all the Holiday Five, Maddy felt the least close to Erin, probably because at camp, Erin had teased her about how much she ate. Now, however, with her resolve to start a diet of her own instead of her mother's, Maddy felt a small glimmer of an urge to share her plan.

"See, my grandpa told my mother I'd lose weight when I was ready. And now I'm ready."

"Do you know what kind of diet you're going to go on?" Jeanne asked.

Maddy waved her hand vaguely. "Oh, the stop-eating diet, I guess."

Jeanne frowned. "That's not a very good idea. You don't want to get anorexic and waste away to nothing."

"Jeanne, I've got a long way to go before that happens." Maddy's brow creased with worry. "I'm not even sure I can stay on a diet. I never have before."

"Well, like you said, you didn't want to before."

Maddy brightened. "Yeah, of course. Now I've got motivation." Maddy was proud of that word. Her mother always used it about going to the gym. "I've got to work out," she'd tell Maddy. "My motivation is fear. Fear of looking into the mirror and seeing a big fat behind."

Maddy was glad that her motivation was going to be love, not fear. *Love.* The word sounded funny even swimming around in her brain. To drown it, she refocused on Jeanne and said, "Guess what, I may have found someone for my mom."

"Tell me," Jeanne squealed.

Maddy spent a few minutes catching Jeanne up on that topic. Then Jeanne looked up at the library clock.

"I have to go to my locker before music. Do you want to come?"

Maddy shook her head. Jeanne's locker was at the other end of the school. After Jeanne left, Maddy wandered around the library. She found a new book on horses and riding and went over to Mrs. Drake's desk to check it out.

"What are you reading?" a voice behind her asked.

Maddy whirled around. "Oh, hi, Mickey," she said nervously. "Ah ... it's a book about horses. I like horses." How lame, Maddy thought. She sounded like a six-year-old.

"Do you ride?" Mickey asked.

Maddy nodded.

"I've never even seen a horse, except in books, of course."

There was a silence. Maddy tried frantically to think of something to say. She had imagined a lot of conversations in the privacy of her room. They had gone much more easily than this one.

"Linda had fun on Saturday," Mickey finally said.

"She's cute."

Mickey nodded. "She can be a pain, but yeah, I guess she's cute."

Mrs. Drake came over to the checkout counter. "I see you found our new horse book, Maddy."

Relieved, Maddy handed her the book and watched as she stamped it for two weeks. When Maddy turned back to Mickey, he was gone.

All the way to class, Maddy went over the conversation in her head. Mickey wouldn't even have stopped to talk to her if he didn't like her, would he? But maybe he was just being polite. Maddy felt confused. She wished she were thinner. Then perhaps she'd feel more confident talking to Mickey. She had only had carrots and an apple for lunch, so maybe she'd see results soon.

Dieting was harder than Maddy had thought it would be, she found over the next couple of days. Somehow, she had had the idea that her determination and her feelings for Mickey would be enough. She hadn't factored in what it was like to feel hungry most of the time.

In the past, when she was hungry, she ate. Often, she ate a lot. Now, she was always watching what she put into her mouth: vegetables, fruit, yogurt. She spent more time thinking about food than she ever had when she wasn't watching her calories. It was odd the way this played out. The more she watched, the more she thought about food, and the more she thought, the hungrier she became. Being hungry, Maddy found, put her in a very bad mood.

On Thursday, she came home from school, assuming that she would be alone, but her grandfather was there, in the den, looking through the bookshelves.

"Hi, Pumpkin," he said distractedly. "Your mom said I could borrow that new mystery she was done reading. Do you know where it is?"

"No," Maddy said, throwing down her books on the table.

"Are you sure?"

"What do I look like, a librarian?" Maddy snapped.

Her grandfather turned and looked at her in surprise. "Maddy!"

"I'm sorry," Maddy muttered. She wasn't used to talking to her grandfather like that.

"What's wrong?" he asked.

Maddy sighed. "I'm on a diet. I guess it's putting me in a bad mood. And don't tell Mom I'm dieting. I don't want her to know."

Maddy wasn't quite sure why she wanted to keep her mother in the dark about her diet, but it had caused so much friction between them in the past, Maddy just preferred to let the results of calorie counting speak for itself.

Grandpa nodded. "Dieting can make you kind of snappish. How much are you eating? Or should I say not eating?"

"As little as possible," Maddy replied.

"Well now, Pumpkin, you know that's not good for you. If you keep this up, you're going to get sick."

Maddy tuned her grandfather out. A diet guru he wasn't. She looked through her notebook for her homework assignment.

"Are you listening to me, Maddy?"

Maddy straightened up. "Yes," she said with a sigh. "But I don't get it. First, you tell me I'll diet when the time is right, and now that it is, you're telling me not to."

"No," he corrected. "I just want you to do it the right way."

I want to do it the most effective way, Maddy thought to herself. All she said though was, "Grandpa, take a look at me. I can afford to miss a few meals."

Grandpa patted his own ample stomach. "Guess that's true of all of us. But you're a growing girl. You need the right foods. I'm just growing in one direction. Out."

That made Maddy laugh. Then she said, "Don't worry. I eat vegetables and yogurt." She didn't mention that was about all she ate.

Her grandfather peered at her. "Your face does look a bit slimmer."

"Does it?" Maddy asked with delight. There wasn't

a scale in the house, but she, too, had thought her face looked thinner.

Grandpa patted her on the cheek. "Pretty soon I'm not going to be able to call you Pumpkin. It'll have to be Carrot or Banana."

"Oh, Grandpa," Maddy groaned. He could be so silly, acting more like twelve than she did.

The phone interrupted them, and Maddy rushed over to answer it. It was Lia.

Without preamble, Lia asked, "What are you doing Saturday night?"

"Nothing."

"Good. Then come for a sleepover. My uncle Danny is coming over for brunch on Sunday, and I thought this would be a perfect opportunity for you to check him out."

"That's great," Maddy squealed. "Have you said anything to him yet?"

"Uncle Danny? No. I think we should plan it out together. This might take some strategy."

Maddy glanced over at her grandfather, who was still searching for his book, and lowered her voice. "By the way, you never told me what he does for a living."

"He's a dentist."

"A dentist!" Maddy's yelp was so loud that her grandfather turned to look at her.

"I know, I know," Lia said with a sigh. "It's not my favorite occupation in the world either, but he tries really hard to be gentle," she added loyally.

"I guess it can't be helped," Maddy said.

"I don't think he's going to change professions."

"Not for a blind date." Maddy giggled. She turned toward the wall, so her grandfather couldn't hear. "On the other hand, free dental care is a selling point. My mother might think having a dentist in the family is a great idea."

"Oh, Maddy, I have a feeling this might really work out."

"Really?"

"Really!"

FIVE

Maddy knew it was risky, but she decided she just had to take the chance. With nothing to do on Saturday afternoon, she walked over to the park to see if Mickey and Linda might have gone there again.

On the way over, she tried to think of excuses for her being there, in case she had to offer one. It was warmer, but not so warm she would just be strolling around the park for no reason. Of course, she was trying to get more exercise these days, but she didn't want to tell Mickey that. She wanted him to turn around and just notice one day how svelte she had become. Better yet would be if he never remembered she had been fat at all.

Perhaps if she saw Mickey she could say she had

lost something in the park last week, but that sounded weak even to her own ears. Maybe she could say she was supposed to meet Jeanne. . . . Before she knew it, deep in thought, Maddy found herself in the middle of the park, very near the swings. Her thoughts were interrupted by a young voice.

"Are we going to see those girls again?"

"I don't think so."

Maddy stopped short. There was Mickey, just a few feet away, his back toward her, pushing Linda in the swing.

"Are they your friends?"

Maddy looked for a tree to duck behind. Fortunately, there was a big old oak nearby.

"Kind of."

"They were nice," Linda said in her high, little-girl voice.

Mickey agreed. "One of them, especially."

Maddy was getting incredibly nervous standing behind the tree. Besides, she wasn't entirely sure which was wider around, her or the oak. Maybe she was only half-hidden. Just the thought of that was enough to make her hightail it out of the park without a look back in Mickey's direction.

Back on the sidewalk, her heart pounding, Maddy went over Mickey's words. One girl was especially nice. Which girl? She was the one he went to school with. So that had to mean he was talking about the "one of them" Maddy, not the "one of them" Lia.

Besides, she told herself as she walked along, he hadn't really said all that much to Lia last week, and he talked to Maddy in class almost every day. How would he know how nice Lia was? Why, he had probably forgotten what Lia looked like. By the time she got home, Maddy convinced herself that she had to be the girl Mickey had been talking about.

Excitedly, she got ready for her sleepover at Lia's.

Mrs. Donaldson appeared in the doorway as Maddy was packing her bag. "What do you want for dinner, Maddy?"

"Oh, nothing. We'll probably order pizza or something."

"You're not hungry?" her mother asked with surprise.

Actually, Maddy was famished. She had skipped lunch, too. But if there was a chance Mickey liked her, she wasn't going to start stuffing herself now. "Not at all."

"Well, if that's what you want," Mrs. Donaldson said uncertainly.

"Don't worry, Mom. I'm not going to starve."

By the time Maddy got dropped off at Lia's, she was hoping that maybe there might be some pizza or even leftovers from dinner. She was afraid she *was* going to starve.

Lia didn't seem interested in food, however. She took Maddy up to her bedroom immediately and started planning how they should get Mrs. Donaldson and her uncle Danny together.

"Do you think we should have them meet accidentally?" Lia asked, stretching out on her bed.

Maddy settled herself in Lia's rocking chair. "How would we do that?" she asked skeptically.

"Isn't your mom coming to pick you up? We could invite her in, and then they could meet."

"She wouldn't come in. She would just honk. Besides, my mom is busy tomorrow. My grandfather is coming for me."

Lia looked up at the ceiling. "Darn."

"Are you hungry?" Maddy asked tentatively.

"Me? No. Say, maybe you could make an appointment with Uncle Danny. Then your mother would take you."

"We have a dentist. I don't think my mother would let me change." Maddy's tone turned grumpy. Wasn't Lia even going to offer her something to drink?

Lia turned to look at Maddy. She had caught the edge in her friend's voice. "Is anything wrong?"

"What do you mean?"

"You seem like you're in a bad mood."

Maddy had to admit it. "Yeah, I guess I am."

"What's the problem?"

She couldn't hide the truth anymore. "I'm hungry!" She said it so loudly and emphatically that both girls started to giggle. "Well, I am," Maddy said a little more quietly.

"Didn't you have dinner?" Lia asked.

Maddy shook her head. "Lunch either."

Slowly, Lia looked Maddy up and down. "You're dieting, aren't you?"

"Yeah," Maddy sighed. "I am."

"You look like you lost weight."

Maddy brightened. "I do?"

"Stand up," Lia commanded.

With embarrassment, Maddy got up.

"How much have you lost?" Lia asked.

"I don't know. My mom weighs herself at the gym. We don't have a scale in the house."

"Well, let's go see. There's a scale in our bathroom."

Maddy didn't know whether she wanted to see if she had lost weight. What if she hadn't? But the scale showed a five-pound loss.

"Good for you!" Lia said enthusiastically. "How come you decided to go on a diet?"

Maddy didn't want to confess her real reason. "I don't know. It seemed like time."

"But you can't just stop eating," Lia scolded. "You're going to get sick."

Maddy was feeling a little woozy.

"Let's see what's in the kitchen. I'll make sure you don't go off your diet," Lia grandly informed her.

Lia's parents had gone out for the evening, so the girls had the run of the kitchen. There was plenty of food for tomorrow's brunch, but it was all wrapped in plastic wrap. Under Lia's direction, they found the leftover chicken from lunch, put some lo-cal crackers in a bowl, peeled some carrots, and grabbed a couple of apples, a bottle of diet soda, and two glasses and took them into the family room so they could watch TV while they ate.

Lia moved the remote control around until they found an old rerun of *The Love Connection* on one of the cable channels.

A couple in their twenties were discussing the date they had gone on to an amusement park. The man, a thin guy with a mustache, had had a wonderful time. But the woman hadn't had any fun at all.

"Jim got the screaming meemies on the rollercoaster ride," she informed the host. "I was so-o-o embarrassed."

"That's not very nice," Lia whispered. "She's dissing her date on national television."

Jim must have agreed, because he started to get mad. "Now that I think about it," he said angrily, "Eloise's outfit embarrassed me. She had no business wearing such short shorts."

"What are you talking about!" Eloise squealed. "I have a great figure."

"Maybe you've never had the rear view of yourself that I got," Jim countered.

Even the show's host looked embarrassed.

"I can't stand it anymore." Lia clicked over to a sitcom. "Boy, what makes a love connection anyway?"

On the sitcom, the star and his girlfriend were kissing, making up after a fight.

"They look like they're doing all right," Maddy said, taking a few more carrots.

"They're on television," Lia said scornfully. "I'm talking about real life."

"Well, what about you and Scott?" Maddy wanted to know. "You said you were starting to like him."

Lia's smile was shy. "Yeah. I think it's mutual."

"When did that happen? At Halloween, you two

were all upset because people thought you did like each other."

Lia turned away from the TV. "I don't know. It was the weirdest thing. Here we were, just friends, and then those rumors started at Halloween. It was humiliating, people thinking we left dance class to make out. Well, you remember."

Maddy nodded.

"Then it got straightened out, and Scott and I went back to just being pals. But over Christmas vacation, we spent a lot of time together. At first, we just worked on our stamp collections like always. Then, one afternoon, I dropped a stamp on the carpet, and we both bent over to pick it up, and our heads bumped."

Maddy frowned. "That dosen't sound very romantic."

Lia lowered her voice. "Then he kissed me."

"Wow." Maddy was suitably impressed.

"It wasn't a real mushy kiss, but it was a kiss, all right," Lia said with satisfaction.

"So now you're going together?"

Lia shrugged. "Whatever that means. We still just work on our stamps and do our homework together."

"Any more kissing?"

Lia shook her head so hard her blond braid swung. "Not yet."

Maddy wondered if Mickey would ever kiss her. Now seemed like a good time to confide in Lia about the real reason for her diet.

"Uh, Lia . . ." She stalled, taking a sip of her drink before she continued. "I wasn't exactly telling you the truth before when I said I just felt like starting a diet."

"Oh?" Lia cocked an eye inquiringly.

"I think if I lose weight, Mickey might like me," Maddy said in a rush. She tried to read Lia's expression. Was her dream so far out that Lia would just laugh at it?"

But all Lia said was, "That would be great."

"So you think it might happen?" Maddy pressed.

"I hope so," Lia answered sincerely.

Maddy wasn't totally satisfied with the answer. Why couldn't Lia just say, "Why of course, Maddy, no doubt about it. Mickey will fall head over heels for you, and it's only ten pounds away."

But before Maddy could say anything, Lia said thoughtfully, "When is the Holiday Five going to get together again?"

"We're supposed to do something around Valentine's Day."

"That's perfect!"

"What's so perfect about it?" Maddy asked.

"We could have a Valentine's party. At your house."

"My house? Well, I guess it's time for me to have the girls over, but—"

"No, silly," Lia interrupted her. "Not a party for just us. A party with boys."

A million things ran through Maddy's mind. Would her mother let her? Who would she invite? Would Mickey come?

"So what do you think?" Lia demanded.

"I think . . . it's great!" Maddy said, her enthusiasm growing. "I can ask Jeanne, can't I?"

"Of course. It doesn't have to be just a Holiday Five party."

"Maybe you guys can sleep over the night before and help me get ready."

"Sure," Lia said. "We can decorate your house with valentines and cupids."

An awful thought struck Maddy. "Wait a minute. I can't have a boy-girl party."

"Why not?"

"I've got plenty of girls, but Lia, I don't know if I can round up enough boys."

"Well, you'll invite Mickey, won't you?"

Maddy nodded. Absolutely. What was the point of a

Valentine's party without him? "How about Scott?"
Maddy asked. "Would he come?"

Lia's face lit up. "Sure. And what about Cal?"

"Cal from camp?" Maddy asked.

"Remember how he monopolized Erin at the camp
reunion? I bet he'd love to be invited."

This party was beginning to sound as if it actually
might be possible. "I could invite my cousin Joel," she
said. "My aunt would make him go."

"Is he cute?" Lia wanted to know.

"He's okay. Maybe he would bring a friend. And
there are a few boys at school I guess I could ask."

"Well, there we are," Lia said, a satisfied smile on
her face. "We'll just check with Erin, Jill, and Kathy
and if they like the idea, the next Holiday Five get-
together will be a Valentine's Day party!"

The next morning, the girls slept in. By the time
they got up, Mrs. Greene was already mixing up her
special waffle batter for the brunch.

"Good morning, sleepyheads," she greeted them.
"How late did you stay up?"

The girls giggled. They had gone up to Lia's room
early enough, but then they had called the rest of the
Holiday Five to ask their opinions about the party.
Everyone thought it was a great idea. After that they

had stayed up to plan the food and the decorations. They had been so keyed up, they had trouble falling asleep.

"You don't even have to answer," Mrs. Greene said, as she wiped her hands on her apron. "But now that you're awake, you can help me in the kitchen."

For the next half hour the girls scurried around, straightening up, setting the table, and peeling fruit for the fruit salad. Maddy got a little nervous as she saw all the food that was filling the kitchen counters. How was she going to resist waffles, and syrup, and melted butter . . . Maddy felt her stomach lurch.

You're just going to have to, she told herself firmly. Whether she would actually be able to, however, remained to be seen.

Maddy was distracted from the food, by the arrival of the company. The first to arrive was a cousin of Mrs. Greene's, Hadley Joseph, who was the guest of honor. She lived in California and worked at one of the television studios in Los Angeles. Normally, Maddy would have liked to listen in on the conversation she was having with Mrs. Greene, but now she was more interested in seeing Lia's uncle.

Maddy glanced out the window. "Lia," she called, "there's some more people coming."

Lia came over to look. "Oh, that's just some friends of my parents. But wait, that's Uncle Danny driving up."

He had a very nice car. A red convertible. Of course, it was winter, and the top wasn't down, but Maddy could already see herself and her mother riding around in the summer.

Maddy watched as he slammed the door and came up to the house. He was tall, with dark hair, and Maddy liked the way he kind of swung his arms as he walked.

"Let's go say hello," Lia said as her uncle rang the doorbell.

Maddy suddenly felt a little nervous. She knew what they had planned for Uncle Danny. He didn't.

"What are you waiting for?" Lia gave Maddy a little push.

Reluctantly, Maddy followed Lia into the hall, where Uncle Danny was hanging his coat in the closet.

"There's my favorite niece," he said, giving Lia a big smile.

His teeth were so white, Maddy noticed, like in a television commercial. But of course, he was a dentist.

"Who's this?" he said, turning his attention to Maddy.

"My friend, Maddy Donaldson. Maddy, this is my uncle, Dr. Daniel Siglin."

"Hello," Maddy said, shaking the hand he offered. "Nice to meet you." But she was thinking, I can hardly wait to introduce you to my mom.

Six

Maddy didn't have to worry about stuffing herself at the brunch. With all the excitement, she barely ate a mouthful.

Before everyone even sat down to eat, Lia pulled Maddy into the kitchen.

"So?" she asked expectantly. "What do you think?"

"He's nice looking," Maddy answered, glancing into the dining room where Uncle Danny was talking to his cousin Hadley. "He might be younger than my mother—do you think so?"

"No, I think they look about the same age."

"Well, that's good," Maddy said. "My dad was the same age as my mom, so that's probably what she likes."

As she helped Mrs. Greene bring the waffles into the

dining room, Maddy reconsidered that. How did she know what her mother liked in men? Except for her dad, Maddy had seen almost nothing of her mother's "type." Mrs. Donaldson could prefer seven-foot clowns with green hair whose noses blinked on and off, for all she knew.

Maddy wondered if her mother ever had daydreams about men, the way she did about Mickey. It seemed hard to believe, but she supposed it was possible. After all, Mrs. Donaldson was always telling her that mothers were people, too.

Lia made sure that Maddy sat next to Uncle Danny at the table. Maddy felt awfully shy, but Uncle Danny turned out to be very chatty and didn't talk down to her at all.

He did ask her about school. Every adult in the world did that. But when he found out she was taking Spanish, he said, "I used to have a Spanish teacher in high school named Miss Fish. She had us call her Señorita, and she wore a rose in her hair."

"Every day?" Maddy asked.

Uncle Danny nodded. "I used to think it was an expensive habit, until I realized the flower was fake."

"Why did she wear the rose?" Lia asked.

"She wanted to look like a Spanish señorita, I guess. But she was in her sixties and she had a double chin." He pulled one of the flowers from the center-piece and stuck it behind his ear. "And she had a very wobbly voice. *¿Cómo está usted?*" he said shakily.

"Danny, are you imitating Señorita Fish?" Mrs. Greene said, frowning across the table.

"Did you have her for Spanish, too, Mom?" Lia asked.

"Yes. And that isn't very nice, Danny."

Danny looked at his sister with a solemn expression, but it was hard to take his apology seriously when he had a daisy tucked behind his ear.

"Same old Danny," his cousin Hadley said. "No wonder you're not married yet."

Uncle Danny sighed. "It's true. Who'd want a guy who imitates his old Spanish teacher, never makes his bed, and doesn't know how to buy clothes because he wears white coats all day?"

"Your mother, we hope," Lia whispered to Maddy. Then she cleared her throat and said, "Uncle Danny, do you ever go out on blind dates?"

"You think I can't get my own dates?" he replied with mock sternness.

"No, it's just that—"

Maddy gave her a kick under the table. This wasn't the time to bring up her mother. Not yet. What if her mother didn't want to get fixed up?

"Well, I just wondered," Lia finished lamely.

"I don't believe in blind dates. They're against my religion."

"I thought you were Jewish," Maddy said to Lia.

Uncle Danny heard that and laughed, but it wasn't a mean laugh.

"Okay, so there's no rule in Judaism about not getting fixed up, but personally, I find it excruciating."

Maddy and Lia exchanged glances. This was a problem.

"But you never know who you might meet," Lia argued. "It could be someone terrific."

"It could be someone horrible," Uncle Danny countered. "And usually is."

"Except, say the person who was fixing you up knew you very well and knew exactly what kind of lady you would like."

"And then, someone else knew a person just like that," Maddy added.

"Then would you get fixed up?" Lia asked.

"I don't think so." He peered at the girls. "What's this all about?"

"Oh, nothing," Lia said, finally digging into her waffle. "I just wondered."

"Sorry kiddo," he said gently. "I've just had some

bad luck with blind dates, so now I'm trying to avoid them."

Maddy stared moodily down at her waffle. The conversation had gone on so long, it was soggy. Normally, she would have just eaten it anyway, but she used its limp appearance as an excuse to have only a few bites. Even that might not have stopped her from gobbling the whole thing, but Mrs. Greene asked Lia to clear the table before she could finish it.

After the table was cleared and the adults were having their coffee, Lia and Maddy escaped to Lia's bedroom for a brief conference.

"Well, that blows that idea," Maddy said, flopping down on the bed. "Darn. I really liked him, too."

"No way I'm giving up this idea. You know what they say about when the going gets tough."

"The tough go shopping?"

"No, Maddy, that's just what they put on T-shirts. The real saying is 'When the going gets tough, the tough get going.'"

"That's nice, but where are we going? Your uncle said no blind dates."

"Not exactly," Lia responded thoughtfully. "He said he didn't think he'd want to get fixed up."

"He sounded like he thought it for sure. Not like it was a maybe thing."

Lia sat down in her rocking chair. She rocked so hard Maddy thought she might tip over backward, but she didn't. "The next thing to do is talk to your mother," Lia finally said, decisively.

"Oh, Lia, what's the point? I don't want to get her hopes up."

"No, no, don't tell her about Uncle Danny yet. Just see how she feels about getting fixed up."

Maddy looked at her doubtfully.

"You don't want to just drop this right here, do you?" Lia asked.

"Okay, I'll ask. But I wouldn't count on us being relatives quite yet."

Driving home with her grandfather, Maddy wondered if she should let her grandfather in on her plan to fix up her mom. She began cautiously.

"Grandpa, remember a while back, when you were telling Mom she should go out on dates?"

"Mmmm." Her grandfather kept his eyes on the road.

"Why do you think she doesn't date much?"

"I don't know. Doesn't want to, I suppose."

"But why doesn't she want to?" Maddy persisted.

Mr. Pappas glanced over at his granddaughter. "I guess I can figure it out. Can't you?"

Maddy thought about it for a minute. "Dad?"

"Your mother was awfully traumatized after your father was killed," her grandfather said seriously.

Maddy tried to remember back to that awful time. She remembered her mother crying a lot right after the car crash, but she also remembered how she went right into paralegal school, and then got a job.

"Mom was sad, Grandpa, but it wasn't like she just fell apart. She always told me we had to get on with our lives."

Her grandfather snorted. "Your mother hasn't gotten on with her life."

"But," Maddy said in confusion, "she works and goes to the gym and . . ."

"And that's about it," Mr. Pappas finished for her. "Work and the gym aren't a life. She needs companionship."

"She has me," Maddy said in a small voice.

"I didn't mean you. I mean male companionship. Even at my age, it's nice to have someone to go out with."

"It's funny you should say that, Grandpa, because I was thinking the same thing. Actually, I might have someone to fix Mom up with."

Her grandfather looked at her with surprise. "You do?"

"Lia's uncle. He's nice. Nice looking, too."

Mr. Pappas shook his head.

"What?"

"Your mother doesn't like being fixed up. I've tried a couple times. She's always said no."

"Have you tried recently?"

"The last time it was Alice who tried. Her neighbor, a guy, a real classy guy named Jack. Your mom wouldn't even go out with him for a cup of coffee."

Maddy sank down in her seat. This was going to be even harder than she'd thought. Maybe when the going got tough the tough got going, but all those tough guys hadn't run into her mother. She could be like a brick wall when she wanted to.

Her mother wasn't home when her grandfather dropped her off, so Maddy decided to take a nap. The late night was starting to catch up with her. She fell asleep before she even had time to pull the comforter off her bed. She awoke to her mother whispering her name.

"Maddy, if you don't get up now, it's going to be time to go to sleep again."

Groggily, Maddy sat up. "What time is it?"

"After five."

It was so dark in the room, Maddy would have believed it was the middle of the night.

With a great yawn, Maddy reached over and turned on the light.

"It must have been some sleepover," Mrs. Donaldson said with a small smile.

Now that she was waking up, Maddy remembered her assignment for the day. Talk to her mother about her love life. Through sleepy eyes, she peered at her mom. She seemed in a decent mood.

"How about a cup of hot chocolate? That should wake you up."

"Do we have the lo-cal kind?" Maddy asked. Then she remembered she didn't want her mother to know how serious her diet was.

But all Mrs. Donaldson said was, "Sure. I'll go down and fix you a cup. Why don't you wash your face. It will wake you up."

By the time Maddy got downstairs, her mother was sitting at the kitchen table drinking a cup of tea, with Maddy's hot chocolate waiting on her place mat.

"So tell me about what you and Lia did," Mrs. Donaldson said as she sipped her tea.

"Oh, we just watched TV last night. Then, this morning, there was a brunch for some of the Greenes' friends and relatives."

"Did you like that?" Mrs. Donaldson asked. "Usually, you're bored with family things. And this family wasn't even yours."

Maddy fiddled with her cup. "It was kind of interest-ing." Maddy took a breath. "Lia's uncle was there. He was telling Lia he doesn't like to get fixed up."

"Smart man," Mrs. Donaldson muttered.

"Yeah, I guessed you didn't like to get fixed up ei-ther. Because you never do, I mean."

"Think about the Chinese water torture. Except in-stead of water dripping on your head, the drip is sit-ting across from you making conversation so boring you want to go out of your mind."

This did not sound promising. However, Maddy was pleased that her mother was talking to her like an equal, not some kid who happened to live in her house. "But what if someone fixed you up with someone they knew was a nice person? Would you go then?"

Mrs. Donaldson looked at Maddy suspiciously. All she said, though, was, "I'm sure everyone who plays matchmaker has the best intentions in the world. There's an old saying: The road to hell is paved with good intentions."

Maddy was getting a little tired of everyone throw-ing old sayings at her today. She decided to change the subject to one that was equally pressing—to her anyway.

"When I was at Lia's we got the idea that the next

Holiday Five get-together should be a Valentine's party. With boys. Here, at our house." She might as well get everything out at once.

"Oh, you did, did you," her mother said with an amused smile. "Well, I suppose we could handle that. We've been talking about cleaning out the rec room. This will give us a good excuse."

Maddy made a face. She knew how much junk there was down in the rec room, but it would be worth it to clean it out if she could have a party.

"How many kids are you planning to have?" Mrs. Donaldson asked.

"Maybe six girls and six boys."

Mrs. Donaldson nodded. "That sounds all right. We can even set the Ping-Pong table up. Oh, speaking of boys, a boy called you this morning."

"A boy?" Maddy sat up straight. "Who?"

"Mickey something. I left his number by the phone in the den."

Mickey had called her! She could hardly believe it. "Did he say what he wanted?" Maddy asked.

"Nope. He just wanted you to call when you came home."

Maddy looked at the clock over the fridge. "I suppose I could call now."

"Now would probably be good," Mrs. Donaldson

said. Maddy could tell from the way her lips twitched, she was trying not to smile.

"I think I'll go in the den and make the call," Maddy said, with as much dignity as she could muster.

"Fine. I'm going to start making dinner, so you'll have your privacy."

Maddy went into the den. There was Mickey's number written down on the pad next to the telephone, but Maddy had absolutely no desire to make the call. No, she would have preferred running back upstairs to her bedroom and pulling the covers over her head.

There were too many things to think about. What if his mother answered? Would she know that Maddy was just returning Mickey's call? If he answered, should she just say, 'This is Maddy'? Or 'Hi, I got your message'? But most important, why was Mickey calling her?

Maddy supposed there was just one way to find out. Shakily, she dialed Mickey's number.

She breathed a little sigh of relief when Mickey answered. "Hi, Mickey. It's Maddy. You called me?"

That was dumb, she scolded herself. Surely he must remember that he called her. But Mickey didn't seem to notice anything amiss. He sounded friendly enough when he said, "Yeah. I'm having trouble with that math assignment, and I know it's your best subject."

Maddy was pleased that Mickey had remembered. "Do you want me to try and explain it to you?" she asked.

"Yeah, that would be great."

They both got out their math books and Maddy tried to talk Mickey through the problems, but it wasn't working very well. Tentatively, she asked if he wanted to come over. "Maybe it would be easier if I could actually show you how to do the equations."

There were a few seconds of silence, and Maddy thought she had blown it. Then Mickey said, "What time's good for you?"

Any time, Maddy thought dreamily.

SEVEN

Maddy didn't know whether she should act casual about the whole thing or go running into the kitchen screaming, "Mom, Mom, guess who's coming to our house"—which was what she felt like doing.

She opted for casual, and forced herself to stroll into the kitchen. "Mom," she said, in as dignified a voice as she could muster, "a friend of mine is coming over for help with his math. Is that okay?"

Mrs. Donaldson turned away from unloading the dishwasher. "Do you mean Mickey? The boy who called?"

Maddy nodded.

Mrs. Donaldson went back to the dishwasher. "What time is he coming?"

Maddy couldn't believe her mother was taking the

news of a male visitor so casually. This was, after all, the first time a boy had come to see Maddy. Of course, math homework wasn't the most romantic reason in the world for a visit, but maybe that wasn't even Mickey's real reason for wangling an invitation.

"I told him to come about seven. We'll have finished dinner by then, right?" Maddy asked anxiously. Not that she actually planned to eat anything, but she didn't want Mickey to think he was interrupting their meal.

"We can eat whenever you like. I was just planning on heating up some stew I made yesterday."

"Stew, great!" Maddy said, before dashing upstairs to plan what she'd be wearing. Stew was one of her least favorite things in the world. She wouldn't be tempted to eat much of the stew at all.

Slamming the door to her room so hard the mirror on the back of it shook, Maddy went toward her closet, but then turned and faced the mirror. Did she really look any thinner? she wondered. Lia said she did, but maybe she was only being polite.

Maddy turned slowly in front of the mirror. Perhaps her stomach didn't stick out quite so much. She peered at her face. It looked a little thinner. Maddy sat down on her bed, discouraged. Five pounds might have been lost, but it would take ten or so more along with them before she got in the normal range. After being so high about Mickey's coming over, Maddy now felt lower than a snake's belly. Why did he have to come tonight? Couldn't he wait to have trouble with his math homework until she looked more presentable?

Well, there was nothing to do but make the best of it, Maddy supposed. She could hardly call him back and tell him that she had changed her mind or that she didn't understand the assignment after all.

Maddy finally got up and trudged over to her closet. If she could find the right outfit, maybe she could get her confidence up. After rifling through her clothes, Maddy decided that the right outfit did not exist. Not in this closet anyway.

Her mother's voice called her down to dinner. As she stomped downstairs, all the days of hunger, and the worry about clothes, and the nervousness about Mickey's visit coalesced into one very bad mood. Mrs. Donaldson had only to look at Maddy's thundercloud expression to ask, "What's wrong?"

"Nothing." Maddy plopped down at her place.

Her mother had put the stew and the salad on one plate, and immediately Maddy grumbled, "You know how I hate it when you put my salad right next to runny stew."

"I know that you didn't like the foods on your plate to touch when you were six, but I thought you had outgrown that particular idiosyncrasy."

"Well, I haven't," Maddy muttered.

"Try," Mrs. Donaldson said tiredly.

The worst thing, as far as Maddy was concerned, was that she was so nervous she felt like eating to calm herself down. She picked out a couple of pieces of beef and then ate all the potatoes and carrots. It tasted surprisingly good.

Maddy would have liked to eat more, but she was well aware that Mickey would be over in about an hour. There was no point in gaining back the few pounds she had lost. She laid down her spoon before she was really ready to.

Her mother noticed. "I know stew's not your favorite, but don't you want some more? And you didn't even have a piece of bread."

Maddy shrugged. "I'm not that hungry, I guess."

Mrs. Donaldson looked critically at Maddy. "You're not on some crazy diet, are you?"

"Mom!" Maddy was outraged both that her mother had found her out and that she assumed any diet Maddy went on would be crazy.

"Are you?" Mrs. Donaldson persisted.

Slamming her napkin down on the table, Maddy said, "Jeez, all you do is tell me that I should go on a diet, so I try and watch what I'm eating and you don't like that either."

"Maddy, please! I think a diet is a good idea, but you have to go about it the right way."

"That's your way, I guess."

Mrs. Donaldson gave a deep sigh. "You're only twelve. I thought you wouldn't start acting like a teenager until next year."

"I'm precocious."

"Enough, Maddy. All I'm saying is, if you don't diet properly, if you don't eat enough, naturally you're going to be grumpy."

Maddy just glared at her mother.

"Maybe you should just leave the table. I'll clean up. Get ready for your friend."

Maddy knew her mother was trying to make amends, so she said, "Okay, I will." She wasn't feeling any better, though.

Upstairs, Maddy looked through her closet once more. She would look silly if she got too dressed up, so finally, she changed to her best jeans, put on a red turtleneck, and threw a flannel shirt over that. She hoped she looked kind of casual and hip. She also hoped that the shirt might cover up a few of her bulges. At least her jeans felt a little loose. That was something.

For the next half hour, Maddy tried to do something about her hair. Lia often wore her hair in a braid, and Maddy thought it looked nice. Her hair was about the same length, but no matter how hard she tried to braid it, there was always a clump of hair hanging behind her ear. Finally, she just brushed it and put on a head-band.

Then she went down to the den. Critically, she looked the room over. It seemed neat enough. Her mother was a great housekeeper, she had to give her that. Plumping the pillows on the couch and putting away a magazine was all she could do for finishing touches. After that, there was nothing to do but wait.

Mrs. Donaldson appeared in the doorway of the den, a bowl of pretzels in her hand. "I thought you might like some snacks while you're studying."

"Thanks." Maddy was feeling bad about her outburst at dinner. She really shouldn't take all her problems out on her mother. "Mom—"

They were interrupted by the doorbell. "Do you want to get it?" Mrs. Donaldson asked.

Maddy nodded. She hurried to the door before Mickey could ring the bell again.

Snow was beginning to fall, and a light sprinkling had fallen on Mickey's hair. Maddy would have liked to put her hand on his dark hair and brush it off. Instead, she opened the door wider and said, "Come on in."

Mickey stamped his boots on the mat and then took off his leather jacket and scarf. Why didn't he wear something warmer? she wondered. Then she remembered how rundown his house was. He probably didn't have a warmer one.

Maddy brought Mickey into the den, where her mother was waiting. She had guessed her mother would want to meet Mickey, but after a brief hello, she disappeared into her bedroom.

"I hope you don't mind me calling you," Mickey said, as they settled themselves on the couch.

You've got to be kidding, Maddy said to herself. Aloud, she replied, "No, of course not. I'm glad you did," she added shyly.

Maddy would have liked some friendly conversation before the studying began, but Mickey seemed eager to get right to work. Maddy spent the next half hour going over formulas with him and checking the answers of his homework.

"Hey, you're a good teacher," Mickey said, leaning back in his chair when they were finished. "Better than that Mrs. Straka. I can't figure out what she's talking about."

A teacher, huh. It wasn't exactly the way she wanted to be thought of by Mickey, but she supposed it was a start.

"Straka is pretty grim," Maddy agreed.

Mickey grabbed a handful of pretzels. "Well, I think I've got the basics down now, anyway."

"Do you want a Coke to go with the pretzels?"

"Nah, I've gotta leave."

Leave? Maddy thought. Now that the fun was beginning, he had to leave? "How's your sister?" Maddy asked the first question that came to her mind.

"She's fine," Mickey said as he gathered his books together. "How's your friend Lia?"

"She's fine, too. I slept over at her house yesterday. We're planning a Valentine's party." Finally, she got Mickey's attention.

"Oh yeah?"

"Yeah." Maddy took a deep breath. "Want to come? It's going to be here, the Saturday before Valentine's Day."

"Sure, I'll come." Mickey stood up.

"I'll send you an invitation," Maddy told him.

"Yeah, that would be good." He gave her a smile that Maddy knew she would tuck under her pillow and dream about.

"Is Mickey gone?" Mrs. Donaldson asked, coming into the living room after Maddy had seen him out.

"Yes." Maddy flopped down on the couch. She was exhausted, as if she had just run a race, not merely done a few math problems.

"He seems like a nice boy," Mrs. Donaldson said. "Polite."

Polite was very big with her mother. Maddy wondered if Lia's uncle was polite. Lia! She had to tell Lia about this astounding turn of events, and that they had their first actual boy for the party.

"I have to make a call," Maddy said, bounding up.

"Right now?" Mrs. Donaldson asked.

"Right now," Maddy replied, giving her mother a pat on the head as she hurried into the den to make her call. She had completely forgotten how annoyed she had been with her mother earlier in the evening.

Lia answered on the first ring, and Maddy quickly filled her in on Mickey's visit.

"So he came for help with his homework?" Lia asked.

There was something so matter-of-fact about Lia's comment that it made Maddy want to contradict it. "I wouldn't say that exactly."

"No?" Lia asked with surprise.

"Well, there were plenty of kids he could have gone to for help." Maddy knew this wasn't quite true. Still, she wanted Lia to think that there was more between her and Mickey than a few equations.

"So you think he just wanted to come over?"

Maddy paused. "I think so."

"That's great," Lia said enthusiastically.

Maddy should have felt glad that Lia believed Mickey liked her, but she didn't. First of all, she didn't think it was true. Not yet anyway, she told herself. And she didn't like what amounted to lying to Lia. She decided to change the subject. "I talked to my mother about getting fixed up," she said.

"What did she say?"

"Oh, about the same thing your uncle did. That it usually wasn't fun and that it was better to pick out your own dates. Not that she ever does," Maddy added.

"Then it's up to us," Lia said decisively.

"You have a plan?" Maddy asked with surprise.

"Well, sort of. I'm coming up on the Friday night before the party, to help you get ready, right?"

"Right," Maddy responded.

"So I can have my uncle Danny drive me up. Your mother could meet him. She'll think he's nice, he'll think she's nice, and then it wouldn't seem like a blind date when we fix them up."

"Not a bad idea," Maddy said, "but won't it be a problem getting your uncle to drive you up here?"

"He usually comes over here for Friday night dinner. If I ask him to take me, I'm sure he would."

After Maddy hung up the phone, she wandered downstairs. She went into the kitchen and opened up the refrigerator door. She wasn't going to eat anything, but she didn't thinking looking would hurt.

There was leftover stew—in its cold, congealed state, that wasn't too tempting—and the usual assortment of vegetables, condiments, and drinks. Maddy closed the fridge and began looking through the cabinets. A tightly closed bag of cookies with a rubber band around it to keep them fresh. A bag of marshmallows. A box of after-dinner mints. Even the graham crackers looked delicious.

"Hungry?"

Maddy whirled around. Her mother was standing in the doorway. "Not really," she said, turning away from the cabinets.

"Why don't you have an apple. Or a banana. Fruit can really fill you up."

Maddy counted up the calories she had consumed that day. Not very many at all. Maybe she could afford a banana. "Yeah, that's a good idea," she said, grabbing one from the fruit bowl.

Her mother came over to Maddy and gave her a little hug. "You know, Maddy, I'm very proud of you."

Maddy looked at her mother, puzzled. "Why? What did I do?"

"You're trying."

Maddy let her mother pull her close, but she was thinking, Trying? That wasn't such a big deal. When was just trying ever enough?

EIGHT

After a flurry of round-robin phone calls, the Holiday Five decided to let Maddy and Jeanne handle sending out the invitations for the Valentine's Day party, since it was going to be at Maddy's house anyway.

Jeanne was excited about the party and about meeting Maddy's friends. "Now tell me again, who's who."

Maddy and Jeanne were sitting at Jeanne's dining-room table with the invitations spread out in front of them. They were cute. They were covered with hearts and had a little teddy bear in the middle. The cards read, "I couldn't bear it if you didn't come to my Valentine's Party."

"Well, there's Lia—"

"She's the one with the uncle," Jeanne interrupted.

"Right. She's an only child like me and she's really nice. We're inviting her next-door neighbor, Scott, because they're kind of going together."

"They are?" Jeanne said, impressed.

"They've been best friends forever, but now they like each other," Maddy explained. "Then there's Erin. She lives in Chicago, and we have to send an invitation to this boy from camp, Cal, because he likes her."

Jeanne frowned. "Is everyone going to be paired up?"

"No. Not exactly." Maddy hoped that she'd be paired up with Mickey, of course, but she didn't want to say it out loud. She hadn't talked too much to Jeanne about Mickey since their first conversation in the library. It was one thing to tell Lia. She wasn't in school every day to watch the two of them interact. Jeanne had a tendency to get too enthusiastic about things, so Maddy tried to keep Mickey out of their conversations. "There was a boy at camp that Kathy liked, but he lives too far to come, so I don't think I'll send him an invite."

"Kathy's the rich one, right?"

"Very rich. I haven't been to her house, but it's in Lake Pointe, and I hear it's like a movie star's house."

"Wow," Jeanne said, suitably impressed.

"The other part of the five is Jill. She's the ice-skater."

"So that's six girls, including me."

"Right." Maddy sighed. "I wanted to have more kids but my mother said six girls and six boys were about all that she—and the rec room—could handle."

Jeanne was doodling names on a pad. "So you've told me who two of the boys are. What about the other four?"

"How about my cousin Joel?" He was also in seventh grade at their school, though in a different homeroom.

"He's nice," Jeanne agreed. "And we could ask Marty Drescher and Max Johnson. Should I put them down?"

Maddy nodded. "Oh," she said as casually as she could, "I already invited Mickey Torres."

Jeanne looked up from her note pad. "You did? When?"

"I told you he came over here the other night for help with his math homework."

It was clear Jeanne wasn't buying Maddy's nonchalance for a second. "But why didn't you wait and send him an invitation?"

"I don't know. We were just talking and I asked him. He said he'd come."

Jeanne looked at Maddy appraisingly for a few minutes, but she didn't say anything. All she did was write

Mickey's name on the pad. Then she put a big check mark next to it.

For the next half hour, the girls busied themselves looking up addresses in the phone book and writing out the invitations. Since they had plenty, they sent invitations to the other girls as well as to the boys.

When they were done, Jeanne said, "I'm starving!" Then she clapped a hand over her mouth. "Oh, sorry."

Maddy's diet was an example of the way Jeanne could get too excited about things. She had thrown herself into helping Maddy count calories with a passion. Maddy didn't mind too much, because she was more careful to watch what she was eating when someone else was eyeing her intake. But she hated the way Jeanne acted as if no one was supposed to eat anymore just because Maddy was on a diet.

"You can have something to eat," Maddy said irritably. "I'll have a diet Coke."

"I don't like to eat in front of you," Jeanne said as they went into the kitchen. "It seems mean."

It seemed a little mean to Maddy, too, but what could she do? The world shouldn't have to stop eating cake—like the gorgeous-looking chocolate one that was sitting on Jeanne's kitchen counter—just because she was trying to get Mickey to like her.

As they sat down, Jeanne with her cake, Maddy

with her soda, Jeanne asked, "What are we wearing to the party?"

Maddy had discussed just that topic with the Holiday Five earlier in the day. "We decided casual."

"Like school clothes?" Jeanne asked, making a face.

"Well, nicer than school clothes, but not dresses or anything."

"What are you going to wear?"

"Something new," Maddy declared. She had lost a few more pounds, and she wanted to show off her shrinking waistline.

Jeanne nodded approvingly. "I think you should get something new."

"I'm going to ask my mother if she can drive me out to the mall sometime this week. Want to come?"

Jeanne swallowed a bite of cake. "Sure. That'll be fun."

Maddy wasn't sure if her mother would be as enthusiastic about her decision to get a new outfit, but she was pleasantly surprised when she asked about a trip to the mall.

"I think you deserve a shopping trip," Mrs. Donaldson said.

Maddy's grandfather, who happened to be over at the time, pulled out his wallet and handed her twenty-five dollars. "I think you do, too."

"Oh, Dad, you don't have to give her money," Mrs. Donaldson protested.

Mr. Pappas put his arm around Maddy. "Hey, I've only got one granddaughter, and I think she's a pretty good one. Let me spoil her a little bit."

"Yeah, let him," Maddy agreed smilingly.

Mrs. Donaldson laughed. "All right. I can't argue with the two of you."

So the next evening, after dinner, Mrs. Donaldson drove Maddy and Jeanne out to the mall and let them loose.

"You're not going to come in the stores with us?" Maddy asked with surprise.

"No, I've got some shopping of my own to do. You've got money, and I trust the two of you."

Maddy felt a rush of gratitude toward her mother. Sometimes her mom really did understand.

Mrs. Donaldson gave them an hour and a half time limit before they were to meet her in the center of the mall at the food court. The girls made a mad dash through several stores, just looking at things, before they went back to the Gap, where Maddy had seen a couple of things she liked.

"Don't you want me to come in the dressing room with you?" Jeanne asked as Maddy marched in front of her with her selections.

"No, that's all right. I'd rather have you see me once I've tried them on." That wasn't the real reason, of course. Maddy didn't want Jeanne to see her without clothes, even if she had lost some weight. Maddy didn't even want to see herself in the full-length mirror with the bright lights of the store highlighting every flaw. It had been a long time since Maddy had gone shopping.

Without looking, she slipped out of her clothes and tried on a pair of black leggings and a white sweater. Once dressed, she glanced in the mirror, but she didn't like what she saw. Even in a new outfit, she still looked big and bulky.

"How is it?" Jeanne called.

"Bad," Maddy replied.

"Let me see."

Maddy opened the door a crack. "It's not right."

Jeanne couldn't get much of a look, but she said, "It's the sweater. It's too heavy. Try on the shirt instead."

The shirt was long, black-and-white checked, with long sleeves. Right away, Maddy could see it did more for her. She stepped out of the dressing room.

"Oh, that's much better," Jeanne said.

"But is it good?" Maddy asked worriedly.

"Turn around."

Maddy slowly twirled around.

"Terrific," Jeanne said approvingly. "It makes you look slim and, I don't know, kind of sophisticated."

"Sophisticated?" Maddy peered into the mirror. She could see what Jeanne meant. The outfit gave her a very together look. She wondered if Mickey would like it.

Maddy's spirits brightened. In the last day or so, thinking about the party had made her more nervous than excited, but maybe things were going to turn out all right. This outfit would give her some confidence, anyway.

The next couple of days went by in a rush. There had been all kinds of calls back and forth about food and decorations and music. Maddy had helped her mother clean up the rec room, and with the help of her grandfather, they had set up the Ping-Pong table. Nervously, Maddy waited for the RSVPs, and to her relief all the boys had accepted the invitation. With all that was going on, Maddy realized that crash dieting would be stupid. Eating so little just made her miserable and unable to concentrate on all the things she had to do. Reluctantly, Maddy had started to eat a little more, though she was still careful about what she ate. It seemed to be working, and Maddy was sure she had lost at least another pound or two.

On the day before the party, Maddy was both nervous and excited. Jill, and Lia of course, were sleeping
over. The big meeting between her mother and Uncle
Danny was going to take place that night. She hadn't
talked much to Mickey all week, but he had told her as
they left math class that he was looking forward to the
party.

"I'm glad you could come," she said shyly.

"Who all is going to be there?" Mickey asked.

Maddy gave him a rundown of the guest list and
Mickey nodded agreeably.

"You'll know most of the boys," Maddy said, "and
Jeanne and me, of course."

"And Lia."

She looked at him curiously. "Sure, you'll know Lia."

As it turned out, Lia and Maddy's plan for match-
making was working even better than they'd hoped.
Lia's parents had to go out of town for the weekend, so
Uncle Danny was going to drive Lia and Jill up for
sure. Lia was bringing a bagful of decorations, and
paper plates and cups, and she had promised that
there was so much stuff, her uncle would have to help
her and Jill bring it all inside Maddy's house.

Maddy was a little more worried about her own part
in the plan. She had to make sure that her mother was

home at the right time, and looking pretty good. Maddy had racked her brain, but she couldn't think of any reason she could give her mother for dressing up in a nice pair of slacks and one of her better sweaters just because Lia and Jill were being dropped off at eight o'clock.

She started her campaign after dinner.

"The girls are going to be here in an hour or so."

"Mmmm." Mrs. Donaldson was curled up on the couch in the den, reading the newspaper.

Maddy looked at her mother critically. She was wearing jeans and a sweatshirt. Her hair could use a combing, her makeup had faded, and she was wearing her glasses. This would never do.

"Don't you want to . . . freshen up?"

Mrs. Donaldson looked at Maddy over the top of her glasses. "You're not ashamed of your old mom, are you?"

"No, of course not . . . it's just . . ."

"Well, I suppose I could put something else on," Mrs. Donaldson said. "Just let me read for a little while."

Maddy looked at the clock on the table. They did have some time, but Maddy would feel better if her mother was made up and ready, just in case the girls got there early. She busied herself for fifteen minutes or so, then she went back to the den and stood in the doorway.

"All right," her mother said with a small yawn. "I'll change."

Maddy thought about going upstairs with her mother and making a few suggestions, but that would raise too many suspicions. Nervously, she waited until her mother came back downstairs. Maddy gave her mom a big smile. She looked great.

Her mother was wearing her tightest jeans and a sweater, both of which showed off her good figure. She had combed her hair and put on a little lipstick. Impressive, Maddy thought.

"Do I pass inspection?"

"You sure do."

They were interrupted by the shrill ring of the phone. Mrs. Donaldson picked it up.

"Oh dear," Maddy heard her mother say. "How did it happen?"

"What?" Maddy demanded. Her mother waved a hand in her direction to quiet her down.

"Of course. I'll be right over."

"Right over?" Maddy asked, alarmed. "Right over where?"

Mrs. Donaldson put down the phone. "Your grandfather and Alice are babysitting Alice's grandkids. Alice fell and hurt her ankle. It might be broken. Grandpa has to take her to the hospital, and I have to go over there and take care of the children until they get back."

"Now?"

"Well, certainly now," Mrs. Donaldson said, heading toward the closet to get her coat. "You stay here and wait for your friends."

"But Mom . . ."

Her mother turned to her. "Maddy, what's got into you? This is an emergency."

Maddy stood and watched her mother hunt for her car keys. Her mom was leaving, and there wasn't a thing she could do about it.

"I'll see you as soon as I can," Mrs. Donaldson called as she left.

"It'll be too late," Maddy muttered.

Mrs. Donaldson hadn't been out of the house five minutes when Jill, Lia, and her uncle drove up. Sure enough, Uncle Danny helped the girls lug their stuff into the living room.

"Hi, Maddy," he said, giving her a grin. "How are you?"

Lousy, Maddy wanted to say, but she just responded with a weak, "Fine."

Lia was looking all around, obviously waiting for Mrs. Donaldson to make her appearance. Lia must have filled Jill in on the plan, because she was peering toward the kitchen, too.

"Uh, Maddy . . ." Lia began.

Maddy just shook her head.

Uncle Danny put the bags down and gave Lia a kiss on the top of her head. "Well, you girls have fun now."

He seemed surprised to see three such glum faces looking back at him.

NINE

"What rotten luck," Lia said, after Maddy had explained the situation.

"I'll say. And you should have seen my mother. She really looked good."

"Maybe there will be another chance," Jill said.

"This one was hard enough to arrange," Lia informed her.

Maddy led them into the living room. "I'm bummed." She flopped down on the couch.

"Me too," Lia said, sitting next to her.

Jill tried to perk up their spirits. "Come on now. We've got decorations to make, and a party to plan. We just can't mope around here all night. We've got to get to gettin'."

"Jill's right," Maddy said. She turned to Jill. "And I'm being rude. I've barely said hello to you. Hello."

Jill giggled and stuck out her hand for Maddy to shake. "Well, hello to you, Maddy."

Jill was the Holiday Five's only African-American member. Maddy knew that Jill sometimes felt caught between two worlds, because Jill had talked to the girls about it. Jill had both black friends and white friends at school, but they didn't always get along. Among the five of them, though, color didn't seem much of a problem, and Maddy was glad about that because she really liked Jill.

"I haven't even gotten a chance to tell you how great you look," Jill said. "You've lost weight."

"Yeah, I have," Maddy said a little shyly.

"Was it hard?" Jill wanted to know. "I'm lucky, I just skate all my calories off."

"It sure as heck was," Maddy responded bluntly. "If it wasn't for . . . well, I just hope there will be a payoff."

Jill looked at her oddly, but all she said was, "So who are these boys that are coming tomorrow?"

Maddy described them to her. She tried to keep her voice neutral about Mickey, but Jill had good radar. "He's the one you're throwing this party for, aren't you?"

"I wouldn't say that, exactly."

Jill turned to Lia, who just shrugged. It was obvious she thought this was Maddy's secret to share.

Maddy couldn't resist. "All right, I confess. Mickey Torres is this totally awesome new kid in my class." She turned to Lia. "Isn't he awesome?" she demanded.

Lia nodded. "He really is something. Tall, dark, and—"

"Handsome!" they all said in unison.

"I can't wait to see him," Jill said.

"Why don't we go up to my room and start working on the decorations?" Maddy suggested. "I don't think my mom would appreciate all that cutting and pasting in the living room."

So the girls trooped upstairs with the bag full of hearts and cupids and lace. They decided to get comfortable in their pajamas, and then sat around for a while planning what kind of decorations they wanted. Maddy had a heart-shaped picture frame she kept on her dresser with a photo of her favorite rock star. Jill teasingly suggested Maddy replace the singer's picture with one of Mickey, and use that as part of the party decor.

Even Maddy had to laugh at that. "I don't have a picture, but when I get one, I'll make an immediate replacement, and have another party," she promised.

Soon, the girls were busy cutting, pasting, taping, giggling, and catching up on all their news. About an hour later, Mrs. Donaldson stopped in Maddy's bedroom to say hello to the girls. She looked exhausted.

"Did I miss anything?" she asked.

Oh, just the chance of a lifetime, Maddy thought to herself. She glanced at Lia, who seemed to be thinking the same thing.

"How's Alice?" Maddy asked.

"She broke her ankle. She's going to have to wear a cast."

"That's rough," Maddy said. "Were the grandkids any trouble?"

Mrs. Donaldson tried to smile. "Nothing but. They're two and four."

The girls, who had all done some babysitting, sympathized.

"It wasn't their fault. They were upset and they didn't really know me. But frankly, all I want to do is take a bath and get to bed." She looked around the room at the decorations. She picked up one large heart Lia had trimmed with lace and streamers. "This is beautiful. I'm not going to recognize the rec room tomorrow. What time are the rest of the girls coming?"

"Jeanne is going to come over in the afternoon to

help decorate, but the others aren't going to come until the party. You didn't forget they're going to sleep over, did you?" Maddy asked anxiously.

"Six girls sleeping on my living-room floor?" Mrs. Donaldson said dryly. "No, somehow that little fact stuck in my brain."

The girls giggled.

"Well, I'll be at your service tomorrow, but for now, I'll say good night," she continued. "Try to get some sleep. You've got a big day ahead of you."

As soon as Mrs. Donaldson was out of earshot, Lia said, "I'm sure my uncle would like her. They've both got the same sense of humor."

"I noticed that too," Jill said. "I think they would have a lot of fun together."

"Great," Maddy said, getting up and stretching her legs, "but we can't seem to fix them up and we can't pull off a meeting."

"You may just have to leave it to fate," Jill said.

"What do you mean?"

"If it's meant to be, it's meant to be," Jill explained. "At least that's what my mother always says."

"Well, so far it's not," Maddy responded with a frown.

Lia sighed. "I just wish we had been a little better at helping fate along."

* * *

"You did a fabulous job." Kathy looked around the rec room. Red and pink streamers were twisted along the ceiling, and on the walls were all the lacy hearts and cupids that Maddy, Lia, and Jill had worked on last night.

"You guys must have been working on this all day," Erin said.

"Practically all day," Jill corrected. "We left enough time to change and get ready for the party."

"You look almost as good as the rec room," Erin responded with a mischievous grin. She turned to Maddy. "And you! You're a skinny Minnie."

Maddy knew that wasn't true, but it was good to have Erin say something nice about her weight rather than teasing her the way she usually did.

Kathy and Erin had arrived about a half hour before the boys were scheduled to arrive. Jeanne had come over early, too, so she had met all the girls. Maddy was pleased that her camp friends welcomed Jeanne as if she was one of them.

"So I have one question," Erin continued. "Are we going to play Spin the Bottle or Post Office?"

"You would want to know that," Kathy groaned.

"I knew we shouldn't have asked Cal," Lia teased. "Erin wouldn't be nearly so interested in kissing games if he wasn't coming."

Maddy hadn't thought much about kissing games. "My mom's going to be right upstairs," she said nervously. "My grandfather, too."

"I don't think we should decide that right now," Kathy said. "After all, I haven't seen most of these guys. How do I know if I want to kiss one?"

That was Kathy, every inch the cool sophisticate. Just thinking about kissing Mickey made Maddy's heart pound. She had a feeling that when Kathy saw him, she'd be interested in playing Spin the Bottle too.

Promptly at seven-thirty the boys started arriving. Cal came first, which was good because all the girls except Jeanne knew him from camp. Cal was one of those boys who wasn't shy at all. As soon as Joel and Max and Marty arrived, Cal started horsing around with them. Scott showed up next. He was friendly enough, but he seemed to want to stick pretty close to Lia.

By ten to eight, Maddy was starting to worry. Where was Mickey? Could he have gotten the date wrong? No, she was being silly. He knew it was a Valentine's Day party. When else would it be?

Jeanne came up to Maddy. "Look what's happening."

Maddy had been so busy eyeballing the clock, she hadn't noticed that all the boys, even Scott, had congregated around the Ping-Pong table watching Joel and Max, who were in a furious match.

Hurrying over to the other girls, with Jeanne right behind her, Maddy said, "What should we do?"

"We could turn up the music," Erin suggested. "Then maybe they'd get the idea we want to dance."

"Maybe we should turn up the music and ask them to dance," Lia said. "After all, this isn't the Stone Age. We don't have to wait for them to ask us."

The girls agreed this was a good idea. Jeanne turned up the boom box, but no one wanted to be the first to wander into the boys' territory. As the girls were whispering among themselves, each egging the others on, Maddy saw Mickey coming down the stairs. She felt her heart leap like a high jumper.

"Now, *he's* interesting," Kathy said, following Maddy's gaze.

Maddy wanted to say, "Hey, he's mine!" but that wouldn't have been very cool. Instead, she tried to get up the nerve to go over and greet her most important guest. Before she could get her feet to actually move in his direction, Mickey sauntered over. Apparently he wasn't intimidated by a gaggle of girls.

"Hey, what's happening?" he said, glancing around the circle.

Maddy introduced him to the girls he hadn't met

yet. He smiled hello to all of them, but it was Lia he turned his attention to.

"So how've you been?"

"Fine. How's Linda?"

"The last time we were at the park, she asked if you were going to show up."

"I'm glad she remembered me," Lia told him.

Maddy watched the interchange with increasing dismay.

Mickey looked around. "How come no one's dancing?"

None of the girls said anything.

"Lia, want to dance?" he asked.

Lia looked surprised, but she nodded, and Mickey led her out to the middle of the rec room.

Maddy caught a glimpse of Scott across the room at the Ping-Pong table. He looked as upset as she felt. What was going on here? This wasn't the way it was supposed to be. Mickey was supposed to come in and ask *her* to dance. Or at least give her more than a brief hello.

Mickey and Lia's dancing broke the ice. The other boys came over and began asking the rest of the girls to dance. Scott grabbed Maddy's hand, but as she suspected, he wasn't interested in her dancing skills.

"Who's that guy?" he demanded.

Maddy didn't even bother to ask who he meant. "That's Mickey Torres."

"He and Lia are acting like they know each other pretty well."

Glancing over in their direction, Maddy saw them laughing together. "They met when Lia came over here a couple of weeks ago."

Scott frowned. "She didn't mention him."

They finished the dance in silence. When the next song started, Scott didn't waste any time hurrying over to Lia. Maddy danced the next dance with her cousin. Neither one of them was very happy about that.

That was the way it went for the next half hour. Maddy danced with everyone but Mickey. Finally, it seemed like Mickey was headed in her direction. Certainly, it was her turn; why, he had danced with Lia twice. Maddy stood up a little straighter and tucked her stomach in. She plastered a smile on her face, turned toward Mickey, and then heard her mother calling from upstairs, "Maddy, the pizzas are here. Can you give me a hand?"

Maddy would happily have ignored her mom, but her chance had passed. Mickey had been waylaid by Kathy.

"Great," Maddy murmured under her breath. "Just great."

With the help of Maddy and Mr. Pappas, Mrs. Donaldson got the food downstairs. There were Cokes and salad and pizzas, which Mrs. Donaldson left in their big brown cardboard boxes. The pizzas were sausage and pepperoni and cheese, and they all looked hot and delicious. Maddy knew she should just take a plateful of salad and maybe a small piece of pizza. She had even planned out the night before just how much pizza her diet would allow. She looked around at the others heaping their plates. Mickey was pouring a glass of cola, which he gave to Lia.

Oh, why should I bother, Maddy thought bitterly as she took the biggest piece of pizza she could find. This night was ruined anyway. She stood off in a corner, watching the others mix, and gobbling the pizza as fast as she could, so she could take another piece.

When the cake, with white frosting decorated with hearts, was brought downstairs, Maddy again decided not to limit her portions. She even cut herself an end piece of cake because it had more frosting. Then she scooped a big hunk of ice cream on it for effect.

"Great party, huh?" Kathy said as she poured herself a diet cola.

"Uh-huh," Maddy answered with her mouth full. Then she moved away from the table, embarrassed.

Jeanne found her eating her cake alone, back in her

corner. Looking at Maddy's empty plate, she said, "No diet tonight, huh?"

"Why should I bother?" Maddy replied.

"Just because Mickey is paying attention to Lia . . ."

So everyone had noticed. Maddy was embarrassed that she had even mentioned Mickey to the other girls, when it was so clear he was taken with Lia. He had sat next to Lia while they were eating—with Scott glaring at him from Lia's other side—and now they were playing Ping-Pong.

Defiantly, Maddy took a big bite of the ice cream and cake.

Max and Joel came to the center of the room. "Hey, it's time to start playing some games," Max said.

"Yeah, where's a bottle?" Joel added.

"We don't want to play Spin-the-Bottle," Maddy called from the corner.

Some of the other girls looked at her like she was crazy.

Lia put down her Ping-Pong paddle. "Oh, why not?"

Maddy wondered darkly if Lia was so anxious to play because she wanted to kiss Scott, or Mickey?

Max was already emptying one of the Coke bottles into another and the other kids were gathering in a circle. Maddy would have liked to stomp upstairs, but she knew she couldn't do that. Grumpily, she took her plate of cake and ice cream and sat down next to Jeanne.

"So does anyone know how to play this game?" Erin asked with a giggle.

"You just spin the bottle," Cal said, and proceeded to do just that.

The bottle spun dizzyingly, and then landed between Kathy and Erin.

"I think it's a little closer to Erin," Cal said.

The other boys hooted, and then hooted louder when he went over and gave her a little kiss on the lips. Then it was Erin's turn to spin. There was laughter when it landed on Jill, so Erin spun again and she had to kiss Joel.

Oh lord, Maddy thought, don't let it land on me. I can't kiss my own cousin. It was bad enough dancing with him. But Joel got to kiss Jeanne. Maddy wished there were some way she could stop this stupid game, and as if in answer to her prayer, her mother came down into the basement with a big garbage bag in her hand.

"What's this, as if I didn't know?" she asked.

Most of the kids looked embarrassed. Under other circumstances, Maddy herself would have been humiliated.

"Maybe you guys ought to get back to dancing,"

Mrs. Donaldson suggested, throwing away some of the paper plates.

Maddy got up and turned the music back on. But as soon as her mother was out of the rec room, someone lowered the lights, and couples began slow dancing. Worse and worse, Maddy thought. At least, Lia was dancing with Scott, she noticed. Maddy was afraid she was going to be left alone, but then Mickey appeared beside her.

Don't get your hopes up, she warned herself.

But she was disappointed anyway when he said, "Why is that guy Scott hanging around Lia all the time?"

Maddy looked at him coldly. "They're going out."

"They are?" Mickey responded, a surprised frown on his face.

"They live next door to each other." *And you live up here in Waukegan,* she added silently, *so you might as well forget about Lia. You'll probably never see her again, at least if I have anything to say about it.*

"Bummer," Mickey said.

Her mother had left the garbage bag in the corner, and Maddy began pitching in more of the dirty plates. Dealing with the rivers of ice cream melting over half-eaten pieces of cake suited her yucky mood.

,"How long have they been going together?" Mickey asked, following her around.

"I don't know, why don't you ask Lia?" Maddy said irritably. Was this night never going to be over?

"She didn't say anything about it to me," he murmured.

Maybe if I put away all the food and turn on all the lights, they'll go home, she thought. Leaving Mickey just standing there, Maddy gathered up as much of the leftover pizza as she could carry in its bulky boxes and brought it upstairs.

Her mother and her grandfather were playing chess in the dining room. They looked over as Maddy stumbled and fumbled her way into the kitchen.

"How's it going, Pumpkin?" her grandfather called.

Maddy tried to say, through trembling lips, "Fine," but she couldn't quite choke out the word. Dumping her cardboard boxes on the counter, she ran through the dining room to her bedroom and slammed the door behind her. Alone at last.

TEN

Maddy had barely buried her head in her pillow when she heard her mother knock at the door.

"Can I come in?" she asked.

"No!"

"Please?"

Maddy sat up on the bed. She knew her mother well enough to know she wasn't going to leave without talking to her. "Oh, all right," she said, wiping the tears from her eyes.

Mrs. Donaldson sat down on the bed next to Maddy. "Tell me," she said simply.

Confessing to her mother was hard. Who wanted to discuss boys with a parent? Finally Maddy got the story out. How great she thought the night was going to be, and how awful it had been, thanks to Lia. "I don't know why I ever went on that stupid diet," she finished in a burst. "I lost weight, and Mickey never even noticed."

Mrs. Donaldson shook her head. "I'm so sorry, Maddy. But if that's why you started dieting, you did it for the wrong reason."

"What do you mean?" What could be a more important reason for dieting than getting Mickey to notice her?

"There's only one reason to go on a diet and that's because you want to lose weight for yourself. Not for a boy or anyone else."

Maddy stared at her mom. "What about all the times *you* told me to diet?"

"I've been thinking about that. I was wrong."

Now Maddy really was shocked.

Her mother started laughing, and even Maddy had to smile.

"You hardly ever say that," Maddy told her.

"I know. It's one of my faults, I guess. But now," her mother added more seriously, "you know you have to go back downstairs."

"I don't want to," Maddy responded, half-defiant, half-pleading.

"Think about it. You have to say good-bye to the

boys. And your friends will think it's awfully strange if you just disappear."

Maddy knew that was true. The girls were sleeping over, after all. Unless Maddy wanted to tell them all to go home, she was going to have to face them sometime. They would have plenty of questions if she didn't go back to the party.

She sighed. "I guess I don't have a choice."

"Not really," her mother said sympathetically. Then she added, "You know, we're not done discussing this, Maddy."

Maddy shrugged. Even though she felt better, she was a little sorry about having confided in her mother. She wasn't sure her mom knew the difference between discussing and prying.

Maddy went into the bathroom and rinsed her eyes. As she walked downstairs, she noticed the lights were back on. Well, at least her guests hadn't used her absence to start a make-out session. Actually, the party seemed to be breaking up.

"Maddy, where's my coat?" Scott asked as soon as he saw her.

"Leaving already?"

"My mother's coming to get me," he replied stiffly.

Maddy glanced over at Lia, who was standing in a

corner talking to Kathy and Jill. The boys and Jeanne were watching Mickey and Joel playing Ping-Pong. Only Cal and Erin, sitting on the couch talking, still seemed to be in a boy-girl mood.

"It's upstairs in the closet," Maddy told Scott.

Jeanne came over to Maddy as soon as Scott was out of earshot. "Where did you go? You missed it."

"Missed what?"

"Lia and Scott had a fight."

"A real fight?" It wasn't very nice, but Maddy felt her spirits lifting. "What happened?"

"Well, Scott and Lia were slow dancing, and then Mickey cut in. Scott watched them for a few minutes, and then he cut in on Mickey. Mickey asked Lia who she wanted to dance with, and Scott said, 'Yeah, who do you want to dance with?' and Lia got upset and said she didn't want to dance with anybody."

"Wow." Maddy had to admit that even though she hated the idea of Mickey fighting over Lia, this was pretty big news.

"Then Scott went upstairs and called his mother, and well, you know the rest. Are you going to say anything to her?"

"Lia?"

"Who else?"

"I don't know," she replied, and moved away.

Maddy could feel her emotions tumbling around like clothes in a dryer. She wanted to gloat, wanted to think Lia had gotten what she deserved, and most of all wanted to sustain the feeling she had had just a few minutes ago when the thought of Lia and Scott fighting had put a smile on her face. For a few seconds she indulged herself. Then she thought, This is so mean.

Maddy glanced over in Lia's direction. Lia looked like she was about to cry.

In her heart of hearts, Maddy knew that it wasn't Lia's fault Mickey liked Lia better than her. And despite how she'd been kidding herself, she had probably known that was true all the time. There wasn't one thing Mickey had done to make Maddy think it was her he liked. How could she be mad at Lia for saying yes to a few dances?

Still, she didn't feel like talking to Lia quite yet. Instead of joining the circle of girls, Maddy went upstairs to where Scott was sitting on the couch, just staring into space.

"Jeanne told me what happened," she said, taking the chair across from him.

He sighed. "I was really looking forward to this party."

Maddy didn't exactly know how to make things better, since talking to boys was hardly her strong suit, but she said, "I think Lia feels pretty bad, too."

Scott's expression turned hard. "That's funny. Most of the night she seemed to be having a pretty good time."

"She didn't know that Mickey liked her." It pained Maddy to say it, even though it was true.

"So, she should have told him to get lost, once she found out."

"Maybe she didn't know how."

Scott didn't say anything.

"Should I go down and get her?" Maddy finally asked. It seemed stupid to have Scott miserable upstairs and Lia fretting in the basement.

"Well . . ." Scott wavered.

"I'll go." Maddy left Scott and went downstairs. She marched over to Lia, who was still huddled with the girls. "Scott wants to see you."

"He does?" Lia asked hopefully.

Maddy nodded. "Thanks," Lia whispered before she hurried to Scott.

Looking around, Maddy saw Mickey standing alone, near enough to the Ping-Pong game to pretend he was watching it, but mostly glaring at the floor. She couldn't deny it, Mickey looking so sad and angry at the same time stirred something inside her. Maybe he didn't like her, but she still liked him. To her surprise he caught her eye and waved her over.

So now that she was next to him, what was she supposed to say? "Hi," she murmured hopefully.

"Where's my coat?" Mickey asked.

Well, at least it was a question she could answer. "In the closet upstairs. Want me to get it?"

"Nah, I'll go."

"I'm sorry you didn't have a good time tonight," Maddy said stiffly.

Mickey gave her that ice-melting smile, even if it was on the woeful side. "It's not your fault. I couldn't wait to see Lia tonight, but I guess she had other plans."

"It's hard when someone you like doesn't like you." Don't I know, she added silently.

"Yeah, well, I guess with her living so far away, it wouldn't have been very practical anyway."

"There's lots of other girls around." Maddy didn't mean herself. Not now. Then she wondered why she felt it was her job to make Mickey feel better, when she felt so bad.

"Sure. I guess I'm being stupid."

"It happens," Maddy said. It gave her a little squeeze of satisfaction to agree.

"Where are Lia and Scott now?"

"Upstairs talking."

"Want to walk me upstairs and get my coat?"

Maddy showed Mickey out, a little wistfully, and then said good-bye to the other boys who were leaving. Finally, only the girls and Scott were left. Maddy left Lia and Scott still in the living room and rejoined her friends.

"Boy, that was quite a party," Kathy said, stretching out on the rec room couch.

"It had everything," Erin agreed. "Romance, jealousy, anger. . . ." Her voice grew progressively more dramatic.

"You seemed to have plenty of romance," Kathy noted. "What's with you and Cal?"

All eyes turned in Erin's direction. But all she'd say was, "Like the movie stars tell the tabloids, 'We're just very good friends.'"

"Where's Lia?" Jill wanted to know.

"Right here." Lia joined their circle.

"Is Scott gone?" Maddy asked.

Lia nodded.

"And did you make up?" Erin demanded.

"Yeah," Lia admitted shyly.

"So what was all that with you and Mickey?" Erin continued.

"I don't know. He asked me to dance, and he was nice. . . ."

"And cute," Jill prompted.

"I can't deny that. And it was fun to have two boys paying attention to me, but a few dances weren't worth hurting Scott's feelings."

While they got ready for bed, the girls continued to hash over the evening, though Lia and Maddy didn't participate much in the conversation. As they were unrolling their sleeping bags in the living room, the two girls found themselves alone together.

"I guess you didn't have a very good time tonight," Lia said after a short, uncomfortable silence.

Maddy plopped a pillow down on her sleeping bag. "It was all right."

"I think I owe you an apology."

"What for?" Maddy asked, busily fiddling with her pillow.

"I knew you liked Mickey, and I monopolized him."

An embarrassed Maddy shrugged.

"I should have pushed Mickey in your direction," Lia said, obviously troubled. "That would have been better for everyone."

"I don't think you could have done that," Maddy responded quietly. "No one could have."

"No, I guess not." Lia looked at Maddy. "Are you mad at me?"

"I was, but I realized that was dumb."

"I'm so glad," Lia said, relieved. "I couldn't have stood it if we had a fight tonight, too."

"Don't worry about it," Maddy told her. She was surprised to find she almost meant it.

"Anyway, we can't fight." Lia's smile was a little trembly. "We still have to get your mom and my uncle together."

Maddy finished smoothing out her sleeping bag. She didn't know which was more unlikely, a blind date for her mother and Uncle Danny, or Mickey waking up tomorrow and finding out that it was really Maddy he liked after all.

It took Maddy almost a whole week to recover from her weekend. The next day, she and her mother had to go all the way into Chicago to see a relative who was in from out of town, so there wasn't even time for a nap. Monday, she dragged herself to school, and she was still tired on Friday.

The one thing she hadn't been too tired to do was eat. If her mother was right, and the only reason to diet was because she wanted to for herself, well, then, she just didn't want to. Food seemed to give her the comfort she needed.

Her mother had noticed that each day the cookie jar

got emptier, but she hadn't said anything. Jeanne hadn't been so willing to hold her tongue.

"You're going to gain all your weight back," she said bluntly, as she watched Maddy chow down on a burger and fries during Friday's lunch period.

Maddy shrugged. "So?" she asked, taking another fry.

"So, you worked so hard, you were looking so good. Just because Mickey didn't wind up liking you isn't a reason to get fat again."

Maddy thought it *was* a pretty good reason. But on Saturday, when she put on her new jeans and they felt tight, she thought about what Jeanne had said.

She went over and looked at herself in the mirror. She still looked thinner, but she knew she was piling the pounds back on. Is that what she really wanted, to be fat again? She remembered how good it felt when she was watching what she ate. How good she felt about herself.

Maddy thought about why she had been stuffing herself. Because she was mad, she guessed. Mad and disappointed. But how was eating going to make those feelings go away?

Then there was Mickey. If she was eating to show Mickey she didn't care about him, that was a waste of time. Fat, thin, she knew it didn't matter to him one way or another.

Suddenly, Maddy felt a surge of anger go through her. Well, it did matter to her. She was tired of being the biggest girl in the seventh grade. She could lose weight if she wanted to, she knew that now. And she wanted to, she realized. She wanted to very much.

That night, as her mother was preparing dinner, Maddy told her, "I just want a chef's salad."

"You do?" Mrs. Donaldson asked with surprise.

"I'm back on my diet."

"How come?"

Maddy took a piece of celery from the pile of vegetables her mother was chopping. "Didn't you tell me there was only one reason to go on a diet?"

"Yes, because *you* want to take the weight off."

"Well, I do."

Her mother broke into a smile. "That's wonderful, Maddy. And I'll do everything I can to help. I'll buy the right food and ..." Mrs. Donaldson noticed Maddy's frown. "How about I'll try to butt out unless you ask for my help?"

Now Maddy grinned. "Thanks, Mom."

"But you can't object if I want salad for dinner, too." She grabbed a carrot. "I love vegetables, you know." Mrs. Donaldson bit into the big carrot.

Maddy heard the crack and winced. It sounded like her mother had broken her tooth, and sure enough, Mrs. Donaldson dropped the carrot and grabbed the side of her mouth. "Oww," was all her mother could say. "Owww!"

"Are you okay?" Maddy asked with alarm. "Mom, do you want me to call the dentist?"

It was a little hard to understand her mother's reply. "Aw'll caw."

While Maddy fixed her mother an ice pack and got some aspirins, Mrs. Donaldson tried to get a hold of the dentist, but he was out of town until Monday.

Mrs. Donaldson sat down heavily on a kitchen chair. "I'll never make it until Monday. I feel like I've got knives in my jaw."

Lightbulb-over-the-head time. "Mom! I know a dentist who will see you!"

"You do?"

"Lia's uncle, Dr. Siglin. He's a dentist. I bet he would take care of you. It's an emergency."

Mrs. Donaldson looked torn. Maddy knew that under normal circumstances, she would never go to a strange dentist. Nor would she ask for a favor from someone she didn't know. But a flash of pain crossed Mrs. Donaldson's face, and she said, "Call!"

Maddy hurried to the phone and dialed Lia. As soon

as Maddy heard her friend's voice, she said, trying not to sound *too* happy, "You'll never guess what. My mother broke her tooth on a carrot. It really hurts, and her dentist is out of town."

"You're kidding," Lia squealed. "What a break."

Maddy looked over at her mother huddled on her chair with the ice pack. "Yeah, she's really hurting. Do you think your uncle could see her? Now?"

"Let me call him and get right back to you. Oh, Maddy, isn't this great?"

"Mmmm."

"Is she right there?"

"Yes."

"Call you back."

"She's going to try him right now," Maddy said, as she hung up the phone. All Mrs. Donaldson could do was nod.

Maddy observed her mother critically. She didn't look bad. Lipstick would help, but Maddy didn't think her mother would welcome a call for a little makeup at the moment.

Lia called back in record time. "He was home. He's glad to do it." Quickly, Lia gave her directions to the office.

"Great," a relieved Mrs. Donaldson said when Maddy gave her the news.

"Can you drive?" Maddy asked.

"I'll have to," Mrs. Donaldson replied, putting on her coat. But just then, Maddy's grandfather walked through the door. He took one look at Mrs. Donaldson, asked what was wrong, and then insisted on driving his daughter to Uncle Danny's office. Without waiting for an invitation, Maddy got in the car, too.

Uncle Danny was waiting when they arrived. He greeted Maddy and her grandfather, and then whisked Mrs. Donaldson into a treatment room.

Grandpa sat down in one of the waiting-room chairs and picked up a magazine. Maddy plopped down in the chair next to him. "So what did you think?"

Grandpa looked up with a frown. "About what?"

"Lia's uncle."

Grandpa shrugged. "He's a dentist," he said, and went back to leafing through the magazine.

"But did you think he was nice looking?"

Grandpa sighed. "What's this all about, Maddy?"

Caught. She should have known she was asking too many questions. But Grandpa thought her mother should be dating more, too. Quickly, she filled him in.

"What a little schemer," Grandpa said when she finished. "You didn't put a nail in that carrot, did you?"

Maddy's lips twitched. "No, Grandpa."

"Well, I gotta tell you, Pumpkin, I don't think your

mother or Dr. Siglin have their minds on romance at the moment."

"But—"

"Maddy," her grandfather warned. "Don't let your imagination run wild." Then he went back to his magazine.

Maddy tried to find something she was interested in reading, but the magazines were either about sports or news or teeth. She'd pick one up for a minute, then put it down. She got up and roamed around the waiting room, then she sat down. She leafed through another magazine, then put it back on the pile.

"Maddy," Grandpa said, "you've got ants in your pants."

"Gross. What's taking so long?"

"It hasn't been that long. It'll be a lot longer before they're done."

Maddy wished she had brought a book, but finally she found a fashion magazine that she could look at longer than five seconds. Just when she was getting into an article on tweezing your eyebrows, her mother and Uncle Danny appeared. Her mother, Maddy noted, looked a lot more relaxed.

"Is she okay?" Grandpa asked.

Uncle Danny patted Mrs. Donaldson on the shoulder. "Very brave."

Mrs. Donaldson put out her hand. "I can't thank you enough."

"Don't thank me until the Novocain wears off," he laughed, shaking her hand. "Take some aspirin as soon as you get home."

Maddy couldn't believe it was just going to end like this, with a handshake and a reminder of painkillers. "Dr. Siglin, maybe you could come over for dinner next week," she burst out.

Everyone looked at her.

"I mean, it was so nice of you to come out on a Saturday and all. . . ." Maddy could feel herself floundering. She looked at her mother in desperation.

Her mother's smile was crooked from all the Novocain, but it was knowing, too. She turned to Dr. Siglin. "Maddy's right. I would like to thank you by doing more than just paying the bill."

"You don't . . ." Uncle Danny began. Then he said, "What the heck, sure, I'd like to come."

As they were setting a date, Maddy took the opportunity to give her grandfather a little poke.

Maddy, her grandfather, and her mother walked out to the parking lot. It was cold and crisp and they didn't say anything until they got in the car. Then Mrs. Donaldson turned to look at Maddy, who was in the back seat. "Don't get your hopes up. It's just dinner."

Maddy nodded. But she was going to get her hopes up. If her mother could find romance in a dentist's chair, maybe there was hope for her too. If not with Mickey, then with somebody else. She had years to find a boyfriend, after all. Now, though, all she wanted to do was get home and call Lia.